Billy
and the
GIANT
Adventure

Dedication

This is for all the kids who struggle at school,

or have dyslexia like me.

Never lose hope. Believe!

You have the power to see things in ways

no one else will! Find your way, just like Billy.

The Billy-Boy Way!

Billy
and the
GIANT
Adventure

Jamie Oliver
Illustrated by Mónica Armiño

PUFFIN

Meet Billy and his friends.

Billy

Anna

Jimmy

Andy

Contents

Prologue   1

1. The Day It All Began   5

2. Boonas vs Billy   43

3. Basil to the Rescue   77

4. Battle of the Treehouse   105

5. The Lost City   135

6. Who's Wrecking the Rhythm?   175

7. Billy's Masterplan   203

8. A GIANT Mystery   223

9. Operation Overnight   261

10. Bilfred's Tale   281

11. A Midnight Adventure   297

12. Together Again!   313

Epilogue   326

Thank you!   328

Recipes   331

Prologue

'**R**ight! Who wants a story? Whose turn is it to pick our book tonight?' I asked.

One excited hand shot up – Jesse, as usual – followed by another slightly less enthusiastic response from his twin sister, Autumn.

Jesse loved bedtime stories, especially if it meant that he got to choose the book to read alongside me. Autumn was much less keen. It wasn't because she didn't enjoy stories, but reading just didn't come as easily to her as it did to her brother. I understood exactly how she felt, but I didn't want her to give up.

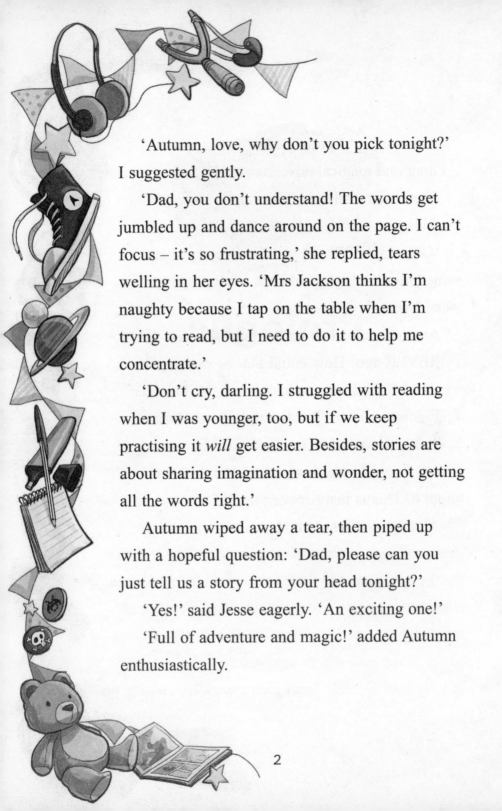

'Autumn, love, why don't you pick tonight?'
I suggested gently.

'Dad, you don't understand! The words get
jumbled up and dance around on the page. I can't
focus – it's so frustrating,' she replied, tears
welling in her eyes. 'Mrs Jackson thinks I'm
naughty because I tap on the table when I'm
trying to read, but I need to do it to help me
concentrate.'

'Don't cry, darling. I struggled with reading
when I was younger, too, but if we keep
practising it *will* get easier. Besides, stories are
about sharing imagination and wonder, not getting
all the words right.'

Autumn wiped away a tear, then piped up
with a hopeful question: 'Dad, please can you
just tell us a story from your head tonight?'

'Yes!' said Jesse eagerly. 'An exciting one!'

'Full of adventure and magic!' added Autumn
enthusiastically.

2

'Hmmm . . .' I pretended to think. 'An exciting *and* magical adventure?'

There was a silence full of anticipation from the kids.

'OK, maybe I'll tell you a *true* story about something that happened back in the eighties, when I was about your age.'

Autumn scrunched up her face. 'That's FOREVER ago! How could *that* be exciting?!'

'Hey! You cheeky monster! Listen, I've been saving this story for just the right time. Because really it's supposed to be a secret . . . so you have to promise me that you won't tell anyone about it. This is just between us, OK?'

Autumn and Jesse nodded, and so I settled down to begin my tale.

'Let's get started . . .'

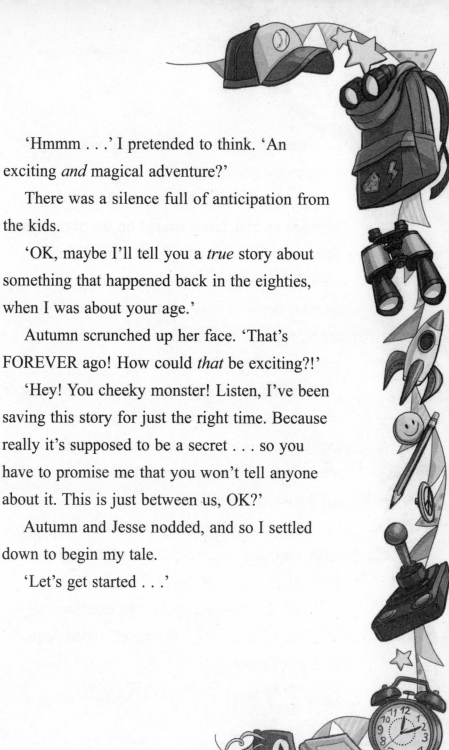

Chapter 1

The Day It All Began

'Billy! Time to wake up!'

Billy snuggled further down under his duvet, trying to shut out the voice that was stirring him from his perfect dream about the most delicious bacon bap . . .

'Come on, Billy. It's Saturday! You know what that means?'

'No school!' Billy shouted, jumping up, all thoughts of sleep instantly forgotten.

'Yup, no school,' his mum said, nodding. She kissed his cheek and pushed his floppy blonde hair out of his face.

In her hand was a plate with crispy smoked streaky bacon in the softest, fluffiest roll, which explained Billy's yummy dream. His mum made the BEST bacon baps! The secret was to have red *and* brown sauce – that way you could dip the roll, muddling the two sauces together to create the most magical taste sensation.

'You know what, Mum?' Billy said with a smile, grabbing the roll. 'I think today is going to be a good day.'

Billy lived in a small village in the countryside called
Little Alverton, with his mum and dad, above a pub
called the Green Giant. It was at the top of the hill that
overlooked the village. Weekends were always really
busy in the pub, which meant freedom for Billy and
usually spending time with his three best friends in the
whole wide world: Anna, Andy and Jimmy. The four had
always been inseparable – they did everything
together: racing each other on their bikes, making up
games together, and just generally mucking around
and having fun.

Billy had known Anna the longest and they had
been best friends from the moment they'd met. Anna
was fearless, fiercely loyal and knew how to make
Billy laugh even when he was in the worst of moods.
Somehow, just being around Anna made Billy feel
braver and bolder.

Andy had been the next to join the gang. Billy
loved that Andy was always himself and happy in his
own little world. Andy was also the only person Billy
knew who loved food almost as much as he did –

although his friend's huge appetite often led to unfortunate, and sometimes explosive, side effects!

Then, a couple of years ago, Jimmy had moved to their village from London ('a Cockney', he called himself – not that the others really knew what that meant) and the three best friends quickly became four. Jimmy was energetic and full of life, but also seriously *obsessed* with nature – so much so that he'd earned the nickname Nature Boy! Jimmy had taught himself everything there was to know about animals, insects and plants and was thrilled to be out of the concrete city he used to live in and finally surrounded by nature.

He'd shown his friends loads of things right on their doorstep that they'd never even realized were there – he believed you could find a garden safari under every leaf and branch. Jimmy's favourite phrase was: 'Look closer and pay attention!' He always said that if you did that you could discover the most amazing things.

And Billy? If you asked his friends, they'd say he was loyal and kind with the biggest heart. He always tried to put himself in other people's shoes and understand how they saw the world. Billy also LOVED tools and gadgets. When he wasn't with his mates he was usually messing about in his treehouse trying to fix broken things or turn them into something new. He might not always end up with *exactly* what he'd planned to make but, even so, Billy's inventions always seemed to come in useful.

It was because of Jimmy's fascination with nature that Billy and his friends had recently made it their mission to discover as much of their village as possible. But there was one area that they were yet to explore . . . Waterfall Woods. It ran along the edge of the village and went on for miles and miles. No one ever went in because it was surrounded by a tall flint wall, which made getting in and out nearly impossible. But, even if the wall hadn't been built, most people in the village would have avoided the place because there'd been tales for years of strange happenings and dangerous creatures.

The stories were made all the worse by old Wilfred Revel, whose garden backed on to the woods. Day after day, Wilfred would stand by the gate of his wonky, run-down cottage – the old gatehouse – and warn people not to stray too far from the road or wander into the woods.

Billy had once overheard his mum and dad talking about Wilfred losing something he loved a long time ago. Billy wasn't sure what they'd meant, but couldn't ask, as he'd have to admit he was eavesdropping! All the children (and some grown-ups) in the village were scared of Wilfred, but Billy wasn't really frightened; he just felt sad that the old man seemed so lonely.

Anyway, about a month ago, there had been a HUGE thunderstorm, and the next day, when Anna had been walking her dog, Conker, she'd discovered a secret way over the wall. The storm had caused an old elm tree to topple over, and Anna – who was always the first one to get stuck into any kind of adventure and loved to climb trees (almost as much as she loved beating the boys at football!) – hadn't been able to resist investigating. She'd found a particularly useful branch that you could pull back, bend and wedge into place while you climbed on to it. Then, when you released it, the branch would catapult you over the wall, where you could gently drop on to a nice soft patch of moss.

Anna had been really excited to tell Billy, Jimmy and Andy about it, and the very next Saturday they'd spent the whole day practising getting over the wall and back again. There was definitely a knack to it, and they all ended up with quite a few scrapes and bruises. Even Andy, with his fear of heights and trees, had managed it eventually – though he took some persuading to actually let go of the branch once he was over the wall . . .

Getting back from the other side had also proved pretty tricky, until Jimmy had the idea of stacking some fallen branches on that side of the wall to make for an easier exit.

They hadn't gone any further that day, but now that they had this nifty way in, Billy had decided that it might just be time for them to explore the woods and find out if the stories were true. With a whole Saturday of freedom ahead of them, today was the day for adventure!

'**Any breakers, any takers – this is Thunderbug looking for a copy. Over.**' *Tscccchhhhh*. Billy's walkie-talkie crackled into life with Jimmy's voice.

It had been Anna's idea to save up for the walkie-talkies (after getting into trouble with her parents one time too many for running up huge phone bills), and Billy had worked out how to link them up to her TV aerial for extra power, range and clarity.

'**Thunderbug, this is Beefburger One,**' Billy said through a mouthful of bacon bap. '**Guys, I think we should go into the woods today. Let's not just bounce over and back – let's explore! Over.**'

'**What about those stories of the dangerous creatures? There must be a reason people don't go in there. Over,**' said Jimmy.

'**Sassy Cat receiving . . . Just got back from my paper round,**' came Anna's voice, clearly out of breath. '**I think it's a great idea! Over.**'

'**Copy, Sassy Cat,**' replied Billy. '**Come on, Thunderbug – we'll be fine if we stick together! Over.**'

'**But . . . Andy's on holiday, so we're not all**

together. Over,' Jimmy countered, still trying to
wriggle out of the plan.

    **'He won't mind. Come on – let's do it! Sassy
Cat, see you at yours in fifteen and then we'll
head to Thunderbug's! Bring some lunch! Over
and out,'** said Billy, signing off before Jimmy could
protest any further.

    Plan agreed, Billy quickly scoffed the rest of
his bap, then raced round his room, getting ready.
He rammed his backpack full of extra supplies
(making a quick stop at the pub kitchen, of course,
to sneakily grab some tasty grub for later), before
running to get his BMX bike.

    It was a sunny day, and he sped down the hill,
away from the pub and towards Anna's bungalow,
where she lived with her adoptive family. Billy was
happily doing bunny hops and wheelies down the
road, singing his heart out (though, to be honest,
wailing might be a better description) when out of
nowhere a half-full bin bag came flying through the air
and smacked him right on the back, covering him in
stinky bin juice. Billy fell off his bike on to the grass,

scuffing his knees and headbutting a tree.

Through a starry haze, he saw a pair of big boots striding towards him, and he looked up to see Bruno Brace, a boy from school who was a known bully. Ironically, his teeth were so wonky that he had to wear a big metal brace to push them back in line.

'Oi!' shouted Bruno. 'Stop riding your stupid bike past my house and stop making that awful noise! It's so annoying! Don't ever cycle past my gate again, understood?'

'Come on, Bruno.' Billy sighed as Bruno towered over him. 'Everyone uses this road; you can't just pick on me.'

'Yes. I. Can!' Bruno growled, giving Billy a shove. 'You're far too happy. You really get on my nerves. Get lost.'

Bruno turned his back and clomped away.

Billy dabbed at his sore, bloody knees, then got back on his bike and cycled on to Anna's.

'Hey, Billy!' Anna said as her friend swerved to a stop in front of her. 'You OK? *Pwah!* You smell a bit funny. And you look a bit sad.'

'I'm fine . . . Bruno threw a bin bag at me – all because I rode my bike past his house singing a bit,' said Billy.

'Why is he always picking on you?! Do you want me to go and sort him out? I'll do it,' Anna said, getting fired up.

'No, let's just forget it and go have some fun.'

'Come on then, Billy,' Anna replied with a smile, giving him a little hug.

The two of them sped off on their bikes, arriving moments later at Jimmy's. An almost picture-perfect house in the middle of the village, it even had a lovely little stream running alongside it. Jimmy was always out by the stream catching stickleback fish, newts, frogs and all kinds of other wonderful things to study.

A few weeks ago, Jimmy's BMX had been squished

by a tractor right outside his house. With Billy's help, Jimmy had done his best to fix it by putting racer wheels on it from his dad's bike, but it looked ridiculous and only lasted a week before it had broken completely, leaving Jimmy totally bike-less.

As his friends drew up, Jimmy jumped on Billy's stunt pegs for a backie.

The friends rode through the village – houses and people a blur as they whizzed along the road. They passed Wilfred Revel's cottage, and Billy spotted the old man standing at his gate as usual.

'Be careful, you lot!' Wilfred cried. 'Keep out of trouble . . .'

The three friends gave each other a quick nervous look, and Billy couldn't help but let out a sigh of relief as the old man's voice faded behind them. However, any anxious thoughts about what might be lurking in the woods were soon forgotten as they reached the elm tree and excitement about the adventure ahead kicked in.

Stashing their bikes out of sight in a ditch, they scrambled on to the springy branch and catapulted over the wall into the woods.

'We need to follow nature's path,' Jimmy told his friends, taking the lead. 'It should take us somewhere really interesting.'

'*Nature's path*? What do you mean?' asked Billy.

'Yeah, I can't see any paths, Jimmy,' added Anna.

'Remember what I always say? Look closer and pay attention, you slimy catweeeeasels!' replied Jimmy, using one of his favourite teases. 'See there, in the undergrowth? There are lots of little paths created by animals using them over and over. Those are the paths of least resistance.'

Anna and Billy squinted at the ground and, lo and behold, they could see interlinked trails leading into the woods made by deer, rabbits and badgers.

'Wow! You're right – look at them all! Let's follow this one,' suggested Billy. He started to head along a well-worn path that seemed to be calling out for him to follow.

'I've always wondered why it's called Waterfall Woods,' Anna said as they walked. 'I've never seen a waterfall around here, and these woods are as flat as a pancake.'

'Probably the same reason our pub is called the

Green Giant,' said Billy. 'It just sounds good. I've certainly never seen a green giant, or any giant, for that matter.'

Not far into the woods, they came to a huge gnarly old oak tree that had a big black scar down the middle of its trunk.

'How come it's all burnt like that?' wondered Billy.

'It's been hit by lightning, but from the looks of it a very long time ago,' Jimmy guessed. 'I reckon it's stayed standing because it's a really old tree – look how wide it is.'

He turned to the tree and did something that Anna and Billy were not expecting . . .

He gave it a big bear hug!

Billy laughed. 'Jimmy! What are you doing?'

'You've got to hug a tree when it's this old. It's mega!' said Jimmy. 'Come on – give it a go!'

Anna and Billy looked at each other and shrugged. *Why not?*

Anna went first, giving it the quickest of hugs because she felt a bit silly. But Billy decided to really go for it, approaching at a run and jumping

with arms and legs outstretched, landing high up and squeezing the knobbly tree with all his might.

Then something incredibly weird happened. As he was hugging the tree, Billy felt an odd sensation zip through his body – like the tingly static shock you get when you rub a balloon and it makes your hair stand on end, or the crackle you feel in the air before a thunderstorm – just for a second, then it was gone. He leapt down from the tree.

'Did you feel that?' Billy asked.

'Feel what?' replied Jimmy.

Billy's friends looked confused. Maybe he'd imagined it.

'Never mind,' he said. 'Come on – let's get going.'

'You know what's weird,' said Anna. 'All this time I thought that Waterfall Woods was pretty flat, but, now that we're actually inside it, somehow it seems different.'

Billy nodded. He'd been thinking the same thing. They'd been walking for about half an hour since they passed the old oak tree and, instead of a flat and even path, they were definitely heading uphill.

'Yeah,' agreed Jimmy. 'Maybe it's some kind of . . . optical illusion or something that means from the outside you can't see how hilly the woods really are.'

'Hmmm. Maybe . . .' said Billy. Was that really possible? That hills could somehow be hidden from sight like that?

They carried on walking, the hill getting steeper with each step. Finally, they reached a clearing at the top, which looked an almost unreal green, giving them a brilliant view of the woods below.

'Does that optical illusion idea of yours explain why the woods also seem so much bigger now we're in them?' Anna asked Jimmy.

'Never mind that,' said Billy, all thoughts of unease gone as his rumbling stomach took over. 'This is a perfect picnic spot. It must be lunchtime by now, and I'm starving!'

They sat down and pulled out their packed lunches. Thanks to Billy's morning raid of the pub kitchen, he'd made sandwiches with spongy fresh bread spread with creamy butter and filled with delicious smoked salmon. Just as he was about to dig in, he realized that Anna and Jimmy were staring at him.

'What's that pink stuff?' Anna asked.

'It's smoked salmon – we use it in the pub all the time. You wanna try some?' Billy replied.

'I don't think I'll like it.' Jimmy grimaced.

'Try it – honestly, you'll love it,' Billy said, as he ripped off two chunks for his friends to taste.

Anna and Jimmy looked at their own sandwiches – ham for Anna and jam for Jimmy – and decided there was nothing to lose, so they stuffed the chunks into their mouths. As they started chewing, suspicion turned to pure joy as the taste of beautiful smoky fish filled their mouths, and big smiles grew across their faces.

'Swap you?' they said eagerly at the same time.

'Oh, come on, guys – you've got your own lunches,' Billy replied.

'Pleeeeeease?' asked Anna with a smile. 'You know you want to, Billy! You dooooo!'

'Oh no, Anna . . . don't!' Billy said, knowing what was coming.

'*You dooooooo,*' Anna said again, giggling. She formed her hand into the shape of a bird's beak and pretended to attack Billy, pecking his neck with it.

'*You doooo!*' Jimmy sang, joining in with a laugh and feeling glad that Billy was on the receiving end of Anna's signature pecking move for once!

'All right, all right – I give in! We can share,' said Billy, passing them some of his lunch.

Anna and Jimmy exchanged smug smiles and gratefully accepted Billy's offering. Anna went to take a great big bite . . .

'Stop!' Billy cried.

'What?' she asked with mild annoyance.

Billy grabbed a lemon wedge from his bag, opened the sandwich and squeezed it over the salmon, before squashing the sandwich back together again. '*Now* try it.'

Anna took a large, satisfying bite – the combination of soft white bread, creamy butter, smoky salmon and tangy fresh lemon was incredible.

'Yum! It's so flipping good!' she exclaimed. She loved it so much that her giant smile stretched from ear to ear.

Just at that moment, there was a loud buzzing noise – **ZZZZZWWWWWWWOOOOOOOOfffff!**

'What's that?' said Billy, looking around.

ZZZZZWWWWWWWWOOOOOOOOFFFF!

The noise grew louder . . . and closer.

Anna let out a yell and pointed in the air, all thoughts of food forgotten. 'Look . . . It's a t-t-t-tiny person!'

'Oh, don't be daft!' Jimmy scoffed. 'It must be a dragonfly or another insect of some sort.'

Billy felt something land on his shoulder. Slowly, he turned his head and, sure enough, sitting there was a miniature person . . . with wings! Billy was astonished.

He couldn't believe what he was seeing. Surely this had to be a dream!

'Close that mouth, young 'un. My name's Basil –
whos is you and whats is yous lot doing in my
woods?' said the creature in a little voice with a
lilting accent.

'Wow! A fairy!' said Anna in amazement.

'Excuse me – I's not a fairy, I's a Sprite,' Basil
said, flying from Billy's shoulder towards Anna.
'Everyone knows that fairies *isn't* real – they is
mythical. But us Sprites, we is magical.'

'But Sprites and magic aren't real either . . .' said
Jimmy, although he had to admit that Basil did seem
to be very real indeed.

'Yeses, we is,' huffed Basil. 'And these is *our*
woods, so never mind whos I's am. Whos is yous?'

'I'm Billy,' said Billy. 'And this is Anna and Jimmy.
We're kids. We're human kids. We didn't mean to
upset you. It's just that we've never seen a Sprite
before.'

'I's never met a hooman before,' admitted Basil.
'So I understands yous being confused.'

That made Billy stop and think. He and his friends
must have seemed as odd to Basil as he did to them!

Billy and Basil looked each other up and down.

'Have you got a tail?' asked Billy.

'No. Yous?' asked Basil politely.

'No. What about toes?' replied Billy.

Basil nodded. 'Yes, toes. Six. Yous? Any wings?'

'Ten toes, no wings,' said Billy.

'Ten toes! That's disgustin'. What yous needs all them for? And what do yous calls these?' Basil asked with a frown, tugging at Billy's T-shirt.

'Clothes,' Billy explained.

'Us Sprites always dress to impress – seasonal fashion,' Basil replied proudly, standing tall with hands on his hips to show off his outfit, which was made from the best that summer had to offer. 'Why doesn't yous wear stuff like this?'

Billy laughed. 'I'm not really sure! I guess we're just different from Sprites, just like all humans are different. Anna's got wavy curls, Jimmy's got tight curls, but my hair's floppy. And you wanna see my dad – he's got no hair!'

'Sprites is all different too – but no hair? He must get nippy . . .'

The air around them started to hum and sway, and in just a few seconds, hundreds – maybe even thousands – of Sprites appeared in the clearing. They tugged at the kids' clothes, pulling and towing the three friends deeper into the woods.

Billy, Anna and Jimmy looked at one another, not sure what to make of this turn of events. It felt like the start of an exciting adventure, but what if the Sprites were up to no good? Billy thought of the village tales of dangerous creatures in the woods. Surely they couldn't be about the Sprites? They all seemed so nice!

'Where are you taking us?' Billy asked with a nervous laugh.

'To our home,' Basil replied. 'We needs to speak to Chief Mirren about yous being here. She's our leader – she'll know what to do.'

Billy, Jimmy and Anna tripped, stumbled and ducked their way through the trees, guided all the way by the flurry of Sprites. The woods seemed to go on forever in all directions, like a completely different world. Billy had wanted to explore, and they were certainly doing that!

Suddenly the Sprites stopped
pushing and tugging.

'We is here,' said Basil.

'Where?' Anna asked.

Billy was confused, too. Basil had
said he was taking them to their home,
but there was no sign of any kind of village or town.

'Remember to *really* look,' Jimmy said, staring at
something in the trees.

'You is right,' Basil said to Jimmy. 'The best
things is hidden till you really tries to see them.'

Billy looked harder at the trees in front of them,
and all at once he started to make out the most
beautiful little huts made from twigs hidden among
the branches. As more Sprites popped out to greet
them, the tiny houses began to glow with lights and
activity. It was amazing!

'Welcomes!' announced Basil over the shrieks
and yelps of the Sprites, who were pointing at the
children and marvelling over their
giantness.

The kids were equally amazed at

the sheer number of little Sprites in front of them: old ones, young ones, some with hats, some in boots – a whole community emerging from the trees.

Basil was flitting here, there and everywhere, proudly introducing his new friends to as many of his Sprite family as possible.

'We needs to bring Chief Mirren to see yous,' he said, flying down to land on Billy's shoulder. 'But till then, while yous is all here with size on your side, it be unspritely not to give you a job or three.' He winked at them and smiled.

'Of course, we'd love to help!' said Billy.

Anna and Jimmy nodded excitedly, just as keen to see more of this amazingly magical world.

And so the friends got to work.

Billy collected big branches and helped to clear away dense undergrowth, saving the Sprites weeks of lifting and backache. Jimmy helped to shore up dams in the river with rocks, which to the Sprites were as big as mountains, while Anna-No-Fear scooted up trees to help the Sprites harvest the juiciest mulberries from the tree tops. Instead of picking them one by one, she shook the branches from up high, and the Sprites caught all that beautiful berry bounty in their baskets.

'The bestest berries used to be down the valley by the river, but this year they hasn't grown at all,' Basil told Anna as she climbed back down to join her friends.

'Do you know why?' Anna asked.

'We's not sure,' Basil said with a concerned frown. 'It's not just the berries. Other fruit and flowers is not good either. We's managin' to use preserved foods from last year to help with supplies, but if somethin' doesn't change soon, it'll be trouble on the horizon. It's like the Rhythm has gone offbeat.'

'What's the Rhythm?' asked Jimmy.

'The Rhythm is the most important thing of all,' explained Basil. 'It's how we stays alive and in harmony with the woods. We can do what we wants to do and be what we wants to be, but only if we all play our part in the Rhythm. And every livin' creature has their own responsibilities. Us Sprites grinds the lava rock and scatters the minerally dust into the river, so

that it can flow right through the land. And every year
when it floods, all that goodness gets everywhere.
Us Sprites feeds the land, and the land explodes with
happiness and gratitude, and in return it looks after
us,' he said, as he rubbed his belly and gave a whoop.

'So what does yous three hoomans do for the
Rhythm?' he asked.

There was an uncomfortable silence as the three
friends looked at each other and realized they
hadn't thought about the world like this before.
They weren't sure whether they were doing anything
useful at all.

'We're just kids,' said Billy. 'We have fun and go to
school . . . I guess we leave that to the grown-ups, to
be honest.'

'Being young'uns is no excuse,' replied Basil.
'It doesn't matter how old you is. We alls got to respect
the land – everybody and everything has to work
together to keep the Rhythm in harmony. You needs
to be careful, otherwise you ends up like those
Boonas.'

'Boonas?' asked Billy, wide-eyed.

Meeting a village of Sprites was mind-blowing
enough, but now Basil was saying there were other
magical creatures like Boonas, too?

'Yes. The Boonas lives further down the river,
and they's always a bit grumpy, but in the last few
months they has gone wild! They is gettin' a bit
scary, to be honest, even tryin' to trap Sprites. They
says they wants to eat us! We's havin' to be ever
so careful. Chief Mirren says we needs to be on
Sprite alert.'

'Oh no!' said Jimmy. 'That doesn't sound good.'

'I knows. The Boonas' part of the Rhythm is to
pick mushrooms and scatter their spores round the
woods. Those spores grows into thousands more
mushrooms, and they breaks down anythin' dead
that's cloggin' up the forest.' Basil pretended to
choke and wriggled his body. 'In return, the spores
helps new life spring into action.'

He spun round with a kick in the air and spread
his arms wide like a blooming flower, grinning broadly.
Then he stopped and stood very still.

'That means everythin' lives forever because

we's all part of the Rhythm: no start, and no end,'
he whispered.

Billy and his friends shared a smile. That seemed
a wonderful way to look at the world.

'But the Boonas has stopped doin' their part, and
that's no good! And there's more. Other bits of the
Rhythm seems to have gone funny – plants not
flowerin' when they should; not as many bees around;
animals actin' strangely; things dyin' when they should
be thrivin'.'

Basil's face fell for a moment, then he turned to
Billy, Anna and Jimmy with a knowing look on his
face.

'And, by the sounds of it, yous need help with your
part of the Rhythm, too. Maybe that's why yous
stumbled into these here woods. Perhaps the Rhythm
has a plan for you hoomans.'

The rest of the afternoon went by in a blur, but
eventually the happy chaos of the Sprite village
calmed to silence, and Billy, Anna and Jimmy

suddenly sensed that
something special was
about to happen.

They looked up to see a
particularly elegant, slightly
taller Sprite gliding towards them.

'Billy, Anna and Jimmy,
I am Chief Mirren, leader of this
community, and I'm pleased to
welcome you to our village,' the Sprite said in a soft
and musical tone. 'Now, we haven't spoken to any
humans before, so I'm curious to understand how you
found us.'

'I don't know,' said Billy. 'I guess we just followed
nature's path, didn't we, Jimmy?'

Jimmy nodded.

'Well, it's really quite special that you did,' said
Chief Mirren. 'The woods must have allowed you to
find us for a reason, and we're very grateful for your
help today. On behalf of all the Sprites, I would like to
grant you a wish to say thank you.'

The friends beamed at each other. A magical wish!

Anna couldn't get her words out fast enough. 'I'd like a remote-controlled car, please. It's called the Monster Beetle, and I'd love a gold one. I've always, always wanted one.'

Jimmy saw his opportunity and jumped in. 'I want a brand-new bike, please. Not an ordinary bike, a Grifter . . . But can it have a built-in water cannon and a loud siren like a police car?'

'And what about you, Billy?' asked Chief Mirren.

Billy paused for a moment, thinking hard about all the things he'd love for himself. Then he smiled and said, 'I wish that Wilfred Revel, who lives at the edge of the woods, could have a day of happiness because he always looks so sad and lonely.'

Chief Mirren looked at the three of them kindly. 'I see that you each have something you desire. I'm afraid, though, that magic is precious, so I can only grant one wish between you all. Which do you choose?'

Anna and Jimmy looked at Billy, then at each other and nodded.

'I choose Billy's wish,' said Anna. 'That's the best one.'

'Definitely,' agreed Jimmy.

Billy smiled at his friends.

'One wish we have, and one wish we shall give,' said Chief Mirren. 'Wishes are rare, like double rainbows, and a wish to share with someone else is the rarest of all. Billy, your wish is granted.'

The friends waited for something to happen.

'Is that it? No cloud of smoke, no glitter?' asked Jimmy.

'You don't have to see magic to know it's happened,' said Chief Mirren with a small smile. She nodded to a cluster of Sprites nearby, who flitted off. 'But magic like this connects us, and I would like to give you something to symbolize this day and our new friendship.'

Two Sprites returned, carrying an ordinary-looking shard of flint that was attached to a long thin piece of twine.

'Billy, as your wish was chosen, you shall receive this gift,' Chief Mirren said.

The Sprites holding the necklace flew over and tied the twine round Billy's neck, securing the flint in place

with a most complicated knot that seemed to take no
effort on their part.

'All stones have purpose,' Chief Mirren continued.
'They can hold messages, just like water can hold
memories. Think of this piece of flint as a little bit of
all of us. In times of trouble, hold us close.'

Each Sprite pulled a teeny stone threaded on twine
out from under their clothes and held it up in the air.

'Even thoughs we's all different,' explained Basil,
'these stones keeps us alls together. Yous is

connected to us now, whether yous likes it or not,'
he said, chuckling.

'Wow!' said Billy with a big smile, as he stroked the
flint. Anna and Jimmy looked on in awe.

'Now the sun is setting, so you should return
home,' said Chief Mirren. 'Please do not tell any of
your kind about us. We trust that the woods and the
Rhythm have allowed you to find our world, but it
should be you and you alone who hold this secret.'

'Of course,' replied Billy, his friends nodding
furiously in agreement. 'Can we come back and see
you again?'

'If the woods allow it, then you are welcome any
time,' Chief Mirren said, and Basil bobbed up and
down happily.

And, with that, the friends raced all the way back
through Waterfall Woods, following the same path
they'd ventured along earlier, unable to believe the
day they'd just had.

'We've really got to keep this between ourselves,'
said Billy once they were over the wall. 'Twinky
promise?'

He stretched out his little finger, and Anna and
Jimmy linked theirs with his to confirm the pact.

Billy arrived home just in time for tea.

'Something magical happened in the village today,'
Billy's mum said as she dished out a delicious bowl of
spaghetti and meatballs with the sweetest, most
flavourful tomato sauce.

Billy looked up in shock. Could his mum know what
had happened in the woods?

'I saw old Wilfred Revel with a smile on his face
for the first time in, well, ever!' his mum went on.
'He told me that the head of the village bowls club
had called him up to invite him to the club house
tomorrow for cake and a cuppa! Apparently, he's been
wanting to join the team for ages now and they've
finally got a free spot. Can you believe that?'

'You know what, Mum? I *can* believe it,' Billy said
with a smile and a twinkle in his eye. 'I'm starving.
Can we dig in?'

'Wait, just one final ingredient . . .' said his dad,

pulling out a bunch of bright green leaves. He started tearing them over their plates.

'What's that?' asked Billy.

'Gennaro from the Italian restaurant gave it to me. He said it's yummy on pasta. He's even given me some seeds so we can grow more on the windowsill. It's called basil.'

Billy grinned. 'Basil? You know, that does ring a bell.'

He laughed and tucked in with gusto as his parents looked on in confusion, wondering what could be so funny. But Billy didn't mind. This had been a day to remember, and maybe it was just the start of a whole new set of adventures.

Chapter 2

Boonas vs Billy

For the next few days, Billy and his friends were on a high after their secret adventure! They couldn't stop talking about the Sprites and about going back to Waterfall Woods. However, it wasn't long before Billy was brought down to earth with a bump.

Wednesday night was parents' evening at school – something Billy always dreaded, and this time was no different.

As usual, his teachers started their chats with: 'Billy's a lovely boy, but . . .' Then the list of things he was doing wrong seemed never-ending. *He doesn't focus . . . He fidgets too much . . . His writing is messy . . .*

*He doesn't like to read aloud in class . . . He's a big
thinker, but can't get his ideas down on paper . . .*

Billy had tried talking to his parents about how
hard he found school, but he could never seem to
explain it properly. It wasn't that he didn't *want* to pay
attention, but his mind just always seemed to wander.
And the words on the blackboard or in his books just
seemed to dance about in front of his eyes, no matter
how hard he concentrated.

'He does struggle, but he's trying so hard – I know
he is,' his mum explained to every teacher they saw.

Even after parents' evening was over, Billy couldn't stop feeling down that his teachers all seemed to think he was doing so badly. He knew his parents were proud of him, no matter what, and would always say it didn't matter about reading and writing and that he was good at other stuff. Even so, Billy couldn't help but feel like he was doing something wrong. He didn't understand why everyone else seemed to find school so much easier.

'Billy,' said Anna, 'you can't worry about how everyone else is doing. You do things your own way – the Billy-Boy Way!'

Billy wasn't so sure about that. The Billy-Boy Way seemed to mostly involve getting things wrong. But he knew that if anything could distract him from school stuff it would be an adventure with his new Sprite friends, so he just wished the weekend would hurry up and arrive!

On Saturday morning, Billy ran down to breakfast. Today his mum's overnight oats were waiting for him on the table. When she'd first made him try them, Billy hadn't been sure because it was kind of like eating cold porridge, but now he loved them. The oats were wonderfully comforting, with little hits of fruit and crunchy nuts and seeds. His mum said it would set anyone up for the day, so it was exactly what Billy needed for another day of exploring the woods.

'I'm off in a minute,' Billy told his mum as he happily wolfed his breakfast down.

'Hold on, sweetheart,' she said, stroking his hair. 'Before you go anywhere, I want you to sort out the mess in the treehouse. We let you have your base in the old apple tree, but it seems to me that all you've done is take things from the pub and our shed, and not put anything back. I love you to bits, Billy, but I wish you wouldn't always start things and never finish them. Can you please just sort it out before you do anything else?'

'But, Mum –' Billy began.

'No buts. You can go wherever you want – within reason – *after* you've tidied up. Deal?'

Billy's shoulders drooped. He wanted to go straight

to the woods, but it seemed his mum wasn't going to give in. Fine. He'd just have to 'tidy' quickly – Basil and the Sprites were waiting.

Up in the treehouse, Billy rushed around as quickly as he could, sweeping up some leaves that had fluttered through the window and sending a few spiders and a sleepy bee packing. There wasn't time for a proper clean-up, so he just needed to get things out of sight of eagle-eyed parents. Besides, the treehouse might have looked chaotic to your average grown-up, but it wasn't *just* a treehouse – it was actually a fortress carefully prepared for battle. Everything scattered around was ready and waiting to help fend off a horde of ferocious Vikings in Billy's imagination, or a very real Bruno Brace attack.

Billy had rigged the treehouse with booby traps, a fake entrance and plenty of home-made protection. He also had a few lovely old biscuit tins to store things like tinned baked beans, biscuits, sweets, dried fruit and nuts – stuff that wouldn't go off – in case the pub got overrun by hungry punk rockers or aliens who ate all the food in the kitchen. You could never be too prepared! His dad had taught him how to use a little electric hob safely, and Billy loved to heat his beans, then eat them straight from the tin with a spoon – not forgetting a little shake of Worcestershire sauce and some tangy melted cheese.

And, taking pride of place in the treehouse, hanging off a makeshift mannequin made out of old, bent, wire coat hangers, was Billy's special backpack.

He'd been working on it for months, stocking it with all kinds of tricks and tools for potential sticky situations and global catastrophes; he liked to think of it as a portable version of the fortress he'd created at the treehouse. Carefully stashed inside, he had special stink bombs, torches (both handheld and head ones), his trusty catapult, a compass, duct tape and his own version of a Swiss army knife, which his grandad had helped him make with all sorts of weird and wonderful attachments. He'd repurposed a retractable washing line, teaming it with rock-climbing rope and a grappling hook to create a makeshift harness.

He'd painstakingly sewn mini binoculars into the hood of the bag, ready to wear, and also added his parents' old Polaroid camera just in case. Best of all, he had recently been experimenting with a self-inflating airbag made from an old life jacket and a can of his mum's hairspray, which he'd stitched into the shoulder strap for any unfortunate skateboard or bike disasters. It was a lot of stuff, but Billy liked to have maximum gadget options, depending on what challenges might be in store, and he found more often than not that he could still pull off a bunny hop on his bike while wearing it!

It was Billy's pride and joy and ready and waiting for action!

Suddenly Billy felt a sting on his chest.

Ouch! he thought. *Maybe that old bee is cross I kicked him out.*

But when he looked down he saw that his flint necklace was glowing . . . He hadn't been stung – the flint had burned him.

He watched in shock as a little message appeared,
as if someone invisible was etching letters into the
stone:

HELP ME!

Then, as quickly as they appeared, the words
vanished.

Oh no! thought Billy. *The Sprites!*

Now was the time to put his carefully prepared
backpack to good use.

'Beefburger One, anyone receiving? Over,' he
put out across the airwaves, desperately trying to get
Anna and Jimmy on his walkie-talkie for some backup,
but there was radio silence.

**'Beefburger One, anyone out there? Sassy Cat?
Thunderbug?! Over.'**

Nothing.

There was no time to waste – if the stone was
sending a message like that, it had to be important.

Billy took a deep breath. He'd just have to go
by himself and hope he was up to the challenge.
He swung down out of the treehouse and ran to the
side of the pub to grab his bike.

'Billy, wait!' his mum cried, spotting him from the window. 'I've made an epic picnic lunch for you to share with your friends.'

She threw the picnic package out of the window to Billy and he just about squeezed it into his backpack, then zipped it up and jumped on his bike. 'Thanks, Mum! Gotta go – Basil needs my help!'

'Hold on . . . Who's Basil?' she shouted after him, but Billy was already speeding away on his bike, the wheels spinning in the dirt.

There was no time to stop by Anna's or Jimmy's house. Billy pedalled as fast as he could through the village to Waterfall Woods. He skidded his bike to a stop and quickly hid it in the ditch before grabbing the branch of the elm tree and flinging himself over the wall. Jimmy's comments about following nature's path rang in his ears as he zoned in on the trail they'd followed and carefully retraced his steps to the old oak tree, which led to the clearing and the Sprite dwellings.

'Basil!' cried Billy as he reached the village. 'Basil, where are you?'

At the sound of Billy's voice, a whole host of nervous little faces appeared.

'Billy,' they chorused. 'Yous got the message, too! Basil sent it to us alls! The Boonas has got him!'

'Oh no! Basil told us the Boonas had started trying to catch Sprites! How did they get him?' Billy asked, worried for his new friend.

'They used to leave us alone, but now the Boonas has decided they fancies Sprites for their dinners! Early in the mornin', just as the sun is risin' and the dews is settlin', they looks for spiderwebs to make a giant web high up in the trees, like a fishing net! And this mornin' they got Basil, who was on patrol!'

'We'd better save him before he ends up as –' Billy gulped – 'Boona food!'

'He was caught by the Stinkers! A Boona clan that lives down by the river. All ten of them!' said one Sprite, looking scared. 'They has super-sharp teeth and has become very mean. Plus, they is MUCH bigger than us. We can't go with you, Billy – we's no match for that lot!'

'Are they really big?' asked Billy nervously.

He wasn't sure that he was up to a mission like this without backup from his friends or the Sprites. What if he let Basil down?

'They's as big as a porcupoodle,' replied one of the Sprites.

'I don't know what a porcupoodle is,' said Billy. 'How big is it?'

'As big as a snout-weasel,' another offered.

'I don't know what a snout-weasel is either!'

The Sprites looked at one another, then buzzed together to create a shape that was clearly supposed to represent a Boona.

'This big!' they all cried.

The shape was about the same size as a rather large cat, which felt much less scary than the creatures he'd been imagining.

'Great, thank you, OK,' said Billy with a smile of relief.

'The Stinkers lives down that hill,' said one Sprite, pointing along the river. 'You'll sees a really tall, really wide red-barked tree, with a big hole ins the side that looks like it's glowin'. Yous needs to go through the hole into their lair, then yous follows your nose, because Boonas smells ever so bad!'

The other Sprites held their noses and shook their heads.

Billy wasn't sure how he was going to save Basil – but he hoped his special backpack was all he would need.

Chief Mirren appeared at Billy's side. She looked really worried.

'Billy, thank you so much for coming. In the past, we have had no quarrel with the Boonas. They've always been short-tempered, so we've avoided them when possible, but they play their role in the Rhythm just as we do. However, recently they've changed for the worse. Do be careful, but please bring Basil back to us!'

I'm not sure I can do this on my own, Billy thought.

But his mum always said he could achieve anything he wanted if he put his mind to it, and his dad's mantra was that actions speak louder than words, so Billy tried to squash the voice of doubt in

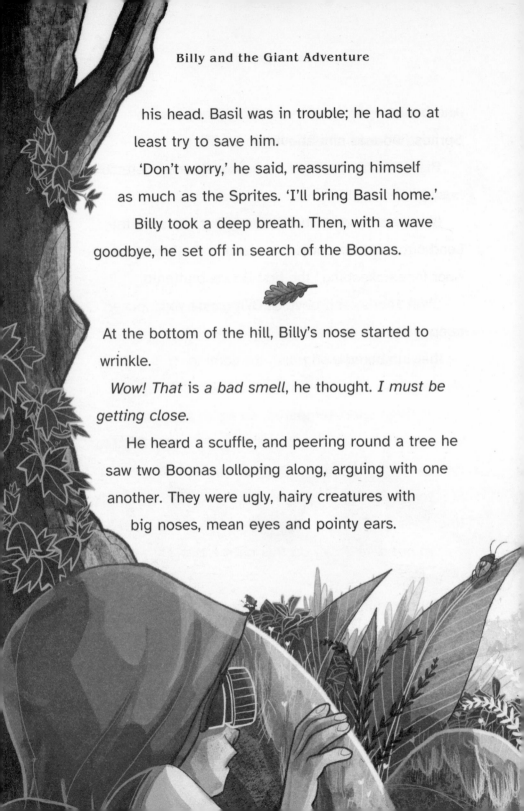

his head. Basil was in trouble; he had to at least try to save him.

'Don't worry,' he said, reassuring himself as much as the Sprites. 'I'll bring Basil home.'

Billy took a deep breath. Then, with a wave goodbye, he set off in search of the Boonas.

At the bottom of the hill, Billy's nose started to wrinkle.

Wow! That is *a bad smell*, he thought. *I must be getting close.*

He heard a scuffle, and peering round a tree he saw two Boonas lolloping along, arguing with one another. They were ugly, hairy creatures with big noses, mean eyes and pointy ears.

And behind them was the glowing tree that the
Sprites had told him about.

Billy held his breath. Luckily, the Boonas were so
busy bickering that they didn't notice him.

'We need to keep that Sprite hidden in case they
send out a search party. I've stashed the key above the
door for safekeeping,' the first Boona muttered.

'Well, that's a bit obvious. Why don't you
keep it in your pocket?' said the second
as they lumbered along.

'I've got a hole in my pocket,' the other replied, clearly annoyed. 'You could have put it in your pocket!'

'I've got holes in my pocket, too.'

'Well, there you go then. The door it is.'

Billy smiled. He couldn't believe his luck. *Step one – get the key. And now I know exactly where to look.*

As soon as the Boonas were out of sight, Billy knew it was rescue time.

The Sprites said there were ten Stinkers – so, if that's two of them, there are eight others somewhere, he thought. *I need to be quiet and quick!*

He delved into his backpack, nudging his mum's picnic aside so he could get his stink bombs ready in case they were needed. He wasn't certain that they'd work, given how stinky the Boonas were already, but anything was worth a try. He also made sure his trusted catapult was easy to reach.

Feeling nervous, and really wishing his friends were with him, Billy summoned up as much courage as he could muster and crept slowly towards the foreboding tree with the red bark.

The glowing hole was easily big enough for a cat (or a cat-sized Boona!) but Billy had to squeeze and bend himself to get through, and pulled his backpack after him.

As he landed on the other side, he gasped in amazement. In front of him was a kitchen filled with little ovens, each with a fire burning under it. Dirty stone pots and wooden ladles littered the muddy floor, and messy wooden plates were piled on top of each other.

Billy tiptoed across the filthy kitchen, feeling like a giant as he ducked to avoid bumping his head on the low ceiling.

He saw a big wooden door with a huge shiny knocker in the middle. It had to be the one the Boonas had been talking about!

He reached up. Sure enough, he felt the key above the door and took it. He shuddered as he realized it was made of bone, then used it to unlock the door.

In front of him was a network of caves and tunnels, damp and dingy, and piled high with all sorts of strange things: boxes, animal skins, giant mushrooms, sticks and pumpkins.

Whoa! These Boonas are definitely hoarders! thought Billy.

He took a deep breath and stepped into one of the tunnels. In the distance, he could hear three, four, maybe five voices all chanting together.

'You're gonna get it, little Sprite,' they said gleefully. 'You're gonna be our dinner!'

Billy crept towards the sound and saw poor Basil in what looked like a pantry store, trapped under an upturned glass.

'Why yous wants to eat me? I's a Sprite! I can help yous with whatever yous needs.'

'No, no, no!' sang the Boonas. 'Sprites are hard to catch. You're a delicacy. Mama Boona's boiling up a stew, and we're going to mash you up and turn you into a fluffy dumpling, then slurp you up with lots of nettles. Yum, yum, yum!'

Billy noticed two of the Boonas leave down a dark corridor and realized that, with just three Stinkers left taunting Basil, this was his moment.

He pulled out his stink bombs and lobbed them towards the Boonas.

'That's disgusting! Was that you?' shouted the first Boona as the smell reached them. He shoved the other two roughly.

'It wasn't me!' said the second one, throwing a punch.

'Your bums are revolting!' said the third, slapping them both.

And, with that, they launched themselves at one another in a fury of fists and naughty words.

It seemed that, even though Boonas were used to their own pong, Billy's extra-special, super-eggy stink bombs were too much even for their noses. Now, when Boonas start fighting and arguing, they just keep on going – they don't know when to stop. Billy watched as the three Boonas bickered and fought, whacking each other and getting in a right old muddle until . . . would you believe it? They knocked each other out!

Brilliant! thought Billy. *They seem to be doing my job for me!*

Not wanting to waste a moment, he sped over to the dizzy Boonas and sat them up, back to back. He grabbed some tape from his bag and bound the Boonas together at their wrists, so even if they did come round they wouldn't be able to move. Finally, he blocked up the corridor the other two Boonas had gone down by shutting the door and wedging some big chunks of wood and branches against it. He quickly lifted the glass from over Basil.

'Oh my goodness, Billy, thanks you!' Basil gasped. 'I can't believe you's here to save me!'

'I was a bit confused when the necklace started to glow and get hot,' replied Billy. 'I thought you were supposed to come and save me, not the other way round. But you called, so of course I came.'

'It works both ways, Billy,' said Basil. 'But that be a lesson for another day.'

'OK,' said Billy. 'The main thing is that you're no longer on the dinner menu. But we can't hang around here. Quick, hide in my bag, and let's get going.'

Basil scrambled into the backpack, and Billy pulled it on. He ducked and raced back through the tunnel and out into the kitchen, slamming the big wooden door shut behind him. He squeezed back through the hole in the tree and landed on the forest floor with a thump. He raced off, as fast as his legs could carry him . . .

Thwack!

Billy was knocked to the ground.

He looked round to see an angry Boona holding a big wooden club. He'd been followed.

'I don't know what you are, but you smell revolting,

all sweet and sickly,' hissed the Boona. 'What were you doing in our lair?'

Billy panicked, his heart thumping in his chest, and doubt rose in him again. *I should have known that I couldn't do this alone. I've bitten off more than I can chew.*

He jumped up, relieved to find himself towering over the Boona, but was still unsure what to do next.

The Boona swung the club again. Without thinking, Billy jumped to avoid being hit, then turned and – like he was taking a penalty in a Cup Final – booted the Boona from behind with all his might. He watched in wonder as the creature disappeared into the bushes.

'That's one–nil to the good guys!' Billy said with a smile.

He turned to carry on through the woods, but another Boona jumped out from behind a tree and pounced on his head!

'Ow!' cried Billy. 'Get off me!'

The creature pulled out a tuft of Billy's hair and grabbed his T-shirt. Billy shook himself as hard as he could, causing the Boona to fly through the air, taking a chunk out of his T-shirt, before crashing into a tree and slumping to the ground.

'Phew!' said Billy. 'Two–nil and hopefully we're approaching the final whistle.'

Then, in the not-so-far-off distance, he heard the first two Boonas returning, still arguing about the key.

'It's not a hiding place if it's the first place you'd look,' scolded one.

As they entered the clearing, Billy scooted up a tree and out of sight. So all the surprised Boonas saw on their return was one Boona slumped against a tree and another with its feet sticking out of a bush.

'What's going on?' said the first Boona.

The other one pointed to a twig on a nearby tree. There, swinging from side to side in the wind, was the bone key.

'How in codswallop did it get up there?' the Boona said, scratching its head.

But, before the first Boona could answer, Billy dropped out of the tree above them, and they all tumbled to the ground. The two Boonas bumped heads as they fell, dropping like stones on top of their sleeping mate.

'Four-nil and the crowd goes wild!' Billy said with a triumphant grin. 'That's what you get for trying to eat my friend!'

'Well done, Billy. But that was a bit close, wasn't it!' came Basil's muffled voice from inside the backpack.

'I know! Are you OK in there?' Billy called over his shoulder to his passenger.

'I's fine,' Basil replied. 'Come on – let's go.'

'Not so fast, you!' interrupted a bellowing voice.

'You don't get away with our dinner so easily! And
what have you done to my poor boys?'

Billy slowly turned round, quickly totting up in
his head how many Boonas he'd accounted for so
far . . . His stomach dropped as he realized there was
one left, and this must be Mama Boona, the one the
others had mentioned in the tunnel. She was, without
doubt, the ugliest, fiercest, stinkiest Boona that Billy
had ever seen – although, let's be honest, he'd never
laid eyes on any until about an hour ago, so he didn't
have much to go on! This Boona was also a good deal
bigger than your everyday cat.

'Now I think you have something that belongs to
me. I'll be having that Sprite back, please – we're
having Sprite stew for dinner.'

She swaggered towards Billy, and he took a few
careful steps backwards.

He turned to run, but in his haste to escape, lost
his footing and fell to the forest floor.

Mama Boona leaned over Billy. She picked up one
of his arms and gave it a pinch. 'There's not much
meat on you, but I bet you're packed with flavour.

Maybe you can make our stew even tastier . . .'

Billy heard some small groans coming from nearby as one of the other Boonas slowly started to come round.

'Come on, boys. Let's get our dinner back to the kitchen!' said Mama Boona, grinning and beckoning the other Stinkers over to pin him down.

Billy was scared and totally outnumbered. He swiftly opened his backpack and scooped Basil out, signalling that his Sprite friend should try to escape. He might end up in the stew, but Basil didn't have to.

Mama Boona had picked up a massive log and pulled it back with all her might, ready to give Billy an almighty whack.

Billy shut his eyes. He'd run out of ideas.

Is this it? he thought. *And with overnight oats as my last meal – what a disaster!*

He had nothing more to give.

Everything felt like it was in slow motion.

Then he thought: *What would Anna do?*

Anna was always the person Billy would go to

whenever he was upset or not sure what to do. She'd tell him to look at things another way, that he was smarter than he thought, and most importantly that he should never, ever give up.

Billy sometimes wondered if Anna was so good at giving advice because she'd been through so much already. She'd been given up by her birth parents when she was just a baby and had been moved from care home to care home when she was little, before settling with her new family in the village. She loved her adoptive family and was very happy now, but the stories she told Billy of all the things she'd already faced were amazing to him.

So now, as the log was about to knock him into next week, he thought about what Anna would do in this situation. He knew that she wouldn't just lie back and become someone's dinner! And what was it she'd said to him this week?

'You do things your own way – the Billy-Boy Way!'

Think, Billy, he told himself. *What is the Billy-Boy Way out of this . . . ?*

Then it came to him. He wasn't without help –

he had his backpack! And Billy had made sure that it was ready for *any* emergency.

He focused in on the little orange cord poking out of his shoulder strap – this wasn't what he'd expected to be using the emergency airbag for, but maybe it could help him out . . . He pulled the cord with his teeth, inflating the airbag, which made contact with the incoming log, which in turn bounced straight back at Mama Boona before ricocheting and taking out the other Stinkers.

Then, to top it all off, the airbag burst, causing a whoosh of his mum's hairspray to freeze Mama Boona's gnarly, matted hair into the most hilarious, ridiculous style. It really was a sight to behold – and it gave Billy a precious second to scramble to his feet and think of his next move.

Basil, who wouldn't dream of abandoning his new friend, was also trying to help by dive-bombing Mama Boona in her dizzy haze.

As Billy stood up, one of his mum's wonderfully round Scotch eggs fell out of his backpack. He snatched it up and lobbed it with all his might at

Mama Boona, watching in wonder as it landed right in her mouth – bullseye! – spewing soft yellow egg yolk all over her warty face. She was totally shocked, but a flash of delicious pleasure also crossed her face as she tasted perfectly seasoned sausage meat. Which is fair enough.

While the Boonas were distracted by the egg attack on Mama Boona, Billy shimmied up the nearest tree, Basil flitting up alongside him and landing on his shoulder.

'What does we do next, Billy?' Basil whispered in his ear.

Hoping the rest of his picnic would prove just as useful, Billy opened the package of food from his mum and began a full buffet onslaught on the Boonas below! He brought Mama Boona to her knees with a double pork-pie hit, then started firing sausage rolls and packets of Hula Hoops (which was a shame, as they were Billy's favourite) at the others, knocking them over one by one.

He looked back into the picnic and saw just what he needed next! Knowing his obsession with Branston pickle, his mum had given him a whole jar of the stuff . . . Billy hastily opened it up and started to fast and furiously scattergun pickle through the air, aiming it at the Boonas' eyes.

With his enemies now in chaos, clawing at their stinging peepers, Billy was ready for his final flourish. He pulled out three fine crunchy apples – intended for him and his friends – and loaded them up in his catapult. He fired two at the last remaining upright Boona, knocking it down like a skittle. Strike! He took a crunch out of the last apple.

'I love it when a plan comes together,' he said to Basil. 'And nothing goes to waste – I see the forest animals are tucking into the picnic food!'

Billy shimmied back down the tree and ran as fast as his legs would carry him, Basil flying alongside him. A huge grin spread across his face. He'd done it! He'd saved his Sprite friend and beaten the Boonas, all by thinking on his feet and doing things the Billy-Boy Way. Wait until he told Anna!

Billy only stopped running when he reached the Sprite village, where Basil gave him the nicest little cuddle on his nose he'd ever had, then sat on his shoulder.

'Thanks, Billy! I's so glad we's friends. If you ever needs help, I's there for you, just like you's there for me!'

'I have to admit, that was a bit tough!' said Billy. 'Please watch out for those Boona traps, Basil. I might not always have such good picnic ammo – you wouldn't have success like that with a jam sandwich.'

Seeing Billy and Basil were back, the rest of the Sprites slowly emerged from the trees and began to joyfully clap and cheer, sprinkling dried petals in the air like confetti.

Chief Mirren flew over to thank Billy for his help.

'You showed immense bravery today, Billy, and

you were true to your word that you would bring Basil back to us. But it is troubling that the Rhythm is suffering such disruption – it's as if it's skipping a beat. Not just the Boonas, but I know Basil told you our food worries. Places where we usually forage are not bearing fruit. The woods feel unsettled and unbalanced, which puts us all in immense danger. It's never been like this before.'

'I can come back with Anna and Jimmy to help you investigate,' Billy said earnestly. 'And if you'll allow it, our friend Andy might be able to help too . . . in some way. We can all help.'

Chief Mirren nodded. 'Thank you, Billy,' she said.

When Billy got home, he found his dad in the kitchen, bent over a big steaming pot on the stove.

'What on earth happened to your face?' Dad asked.

'Oh, I, er, I fell out of a tree,' Billy said sheepishly. The Boonas' attack had taken its toll!

His dad tutted. 'What'll we do with you, eh? You need to be more careful, Billy.'

Billy looked away. If only his dad knew the truth about what had *really* happened today!

'Now go and get yourself cleaned up before we eat, son. I've cooked up a lovely meat stew, and I'm going to plop in these nice dumplings to top it all off.'

'Dad!' interrupted Billy, feeling a bit sick. 'I'm sorry, but I'm not sure I can manage stew and dumplings today . . . I'm, um, still full from Mum's picnic.' It just reminded him too much of the Boonas' plan.

'Really? Usually you're starving come teatime. Your mum must have sent you off with a nice lot of food! Did your friends enjoy it, too?'

'Yeah, they certainly got a faceful,' Billy said, chuckling to himself. 'Maybe I could have something simple for tea instead?'

'Well, all the more for us, I suppose! How does a cheese-and-baked-bean toastie sound to you?'

Billy nodded enthusiastically. Yum! His favourite treat was just what he needed after all the action of the day. He was really proud of himself for finding his own way to do things. Perhaps the Billy-Boy Way wasn't so bad after all . . .

After tea, Billy retreated to his bedroom, eager to get out his walkie-talkie and tell his friends all about his rescue mission. As he shared his story, there was radio silence from his friends, who listened intently before giving him a massive round of applause.

'**The Billy-Boy Way has saved the day! Well done, Beefburger One! Over,**' said Anna.

'**Thanks!**' he said with a smile. '**But listen, there's more. Chief Mirren is really worried about the Rhythm. We've got to help!**'

And once again silence fell as Billy told Anna and Jimmy what the Sprite leader had said. Surely together the three of them – plus Andy – could find out what was behind the problems in Waterfall Woods?

Chapter 3

Basil to the Rescue

The trouble with being nine and a half years old is that, even when you're on a fact-finding Sprite mission, you're still expected to go to school and do your homework.

So, less than a week after his epic Boona battle, Billy found himself sitting in class on Friday morning, trying to avoid the gaze of his teacher, Mr Rogers. He was droning on about the upcoming tests that would decide which sets everyone would be put in for different subjects. Billy hated tests more than anything, and these sounded awful because he was bound to fail and end up being separated from his friends.

He was itching to get back to Waterfall Woods, where school didn't matter and he didn't feel like a constant disappointment.

Plus, he'd nearly got a late mark that morning because he was having to take a slightly longer route to school to avoid a Bruno battering. He had slid into his chair next to Anna just in time for register.

'What happened? You oversleep?' Anna had asked.

'I had to skateboard the long way round – I didn't want to get Bruno'ed again,' said Billy with a sigh.

'I know the feeling,' piped up Scrawny Al, who still had silent tears running down his pink cheeks and a very pained expression on his face. 'I got wedgied really bad.'

'I know the feeling, too,' said Graham, pointing at his hairless eyebrows.

'And me,' said Dexter, smiling to reveal a gap in his teeth.

'You know what, Billy?' said Anna. 'You just gotta rise above it – the best way to get to a bully is to kill them with kindness!'

But Billy wasn't convinced. How could anyone

be kind to Bruno when he was so mean?

Now Billy's attention was dragged back to
Mr Rogers. 'Right, enough about tests,' he said.
'Who wants to do some creative writing?'

Billy's heart sank – he loved making up stories, but
for some reason, when it came to writing them down,
he just couldn't get his thoughts straight and on to
paper. It was even worse when Mr Rogers asked
someone to read out their writing to the rest of the
class. It didn't matter how much Billy tried to sink into
his chair and hide; it felt like his teacher always picked
on him to read out loud, like he could smell Billy's fear.

When would this week be over?

At lunchtime, Billy was in the queue, trying to decide
between a sausage roll and shepherd's pie, while
eyeing up the spotted dick for pudding. As he
collected his food and turned to find a table, he came
face to face with Bruno, who'd been patrolling the
lunch queue demanding that people hand over their
dinner money.

'You again! What – are you following me or something? You know, maybe I should ban you from coming near *me*, not just my house,' Bruno said with a smirk.

Quick as a flash, he picked up the plate of shepherd's pie on Billy's tray and upturned it on Billy's head, like a hat. The canteen fell silent as everyone looked on in horror.

Billy took a deep breath. He felt the tears welling up behind his eyes, but he fought to hold them back, not wanting to give Bruno the satisfaction. He glanced over at Anna and Jimmy, seeking out help from his friends, but then he realized something . . . He wasn't the same Billy he had been last week when Bruno had knocked him off his BMX. He'd fought off a whole clan of stinky Boonas all by himself! So surely he could deal with Bruno Brace without needing backup?

Let's do this the Billy-Boy Way, he thought.

Putting on a brave smile, he stuck out his tongue to taste the food dripping down his face. He turned to the dinner ladies. 'Gwenda, Brenda,' he called sweetly, 'delicious as usual, ladies, but a few more shakes of

Worcestershire sauce might be the way to go.'

'I told you,' said Gwenda, nudging Brenda.

Turning back to Bruno, Billy looked him right in the eye and said, 'Good job our school dinners are a bit cold – otherwise that could have really hurt, but I think this is maybe a good look for me. Thank you, Bruno.'

All the other kids burst out laughing, and Billy walked over to where his friends were sitting.

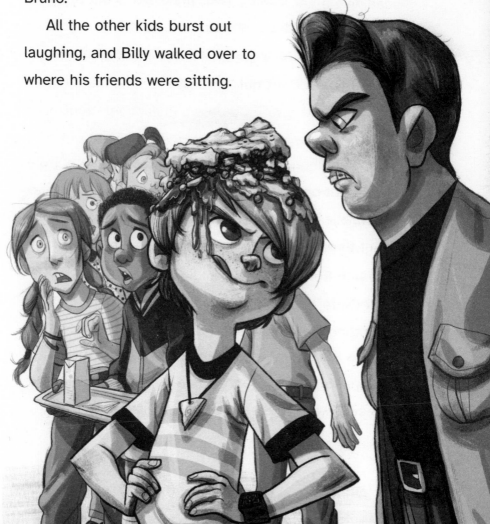

'Nice one, Billy,' said Jimmy.

Billy smiled and took a small, cautious bow.

'This ain't over, you donkey,' Bruno snarled at Billy, his cheeks burning with anger and embarrassment, before elbowing his way through the crowd of watching kids and out of the canteen.

Anna started picking peas and carrots out of Billy's hair. 'See, what did I tell you?' she said with a grin. 'When it comes to bullies, the best way to deal with them is to kill them with kindness.'

Billy was still on a high as he skateboarded away from school. Not only was he going to his grandad's house for tea, but it was a bank holiday weekend, which meant three whole days off school! He'd promised his parents that he'd stop by the village shop to pick up some groceries for Grandad. Billy loved his grandad's house. It was cute and quirky, and the garden led down to the same little stream that ran alongside Jimmy's house. His grandad had so much amazing stuff everywhere – there were loads of trinkets and

gadgets to mess about with and a wonderful old
record player with lots of records to choose from.
Billy would spend ages hanging out with his grandad,
listening to songs and sitting side by side on two
battered old reclining chairs, chatting away. The two
of them were the best of friends.

Billy was especially excited to visit today because
Grandad had lived in the village his whole life and
knew *everything* about *everything*, so Billy was sure
he'd be able to tell him something useful about the
woods.

'All right, son?' said Norman Monk, the shopkeeper,
as Billy walked into the village shop. 'I've got Ted's
bag of bits ready out the back.'

Billy waited by the counter for Norman to grab his
grandad's shopping, in awe of how much stuff the
shopkeeper had managed to cram into such a tiny
space. It was like a library of groceries, and Norman
had one of everything you could ever think of. Glass
cabinets housed Norman's famous bakes next to an
array of 'best in show' awards from the village fair.

He usually sold out of the sweet stuff by lunchtime,

but today Billy spotted a beautifully plump doughnut
sitting all alone in the corner of a cabinet.

Transfixed by the oozy jammy doughnut, Billy's
mum's favourite song – 'Together in Electric Dreams'
by that guy from the Human League – filled his head.
Suddenly the world around him disappeared, and it
was like all the baked sweet treats on the shelves
started dancing along to the song, the flapjacks
providing the backing vocals with harmonizing *oohs*
and *ahhs*, and a pink iced bun playing the synthesizer.
All the while, the doughnut – glistening

with yumminess –

delivered a killer

guitar solo.

'Billy? You're

not listening to me,

are you?' asked

Norman, laughing.

Billy hadn't even noticed

him come back into

the shop.

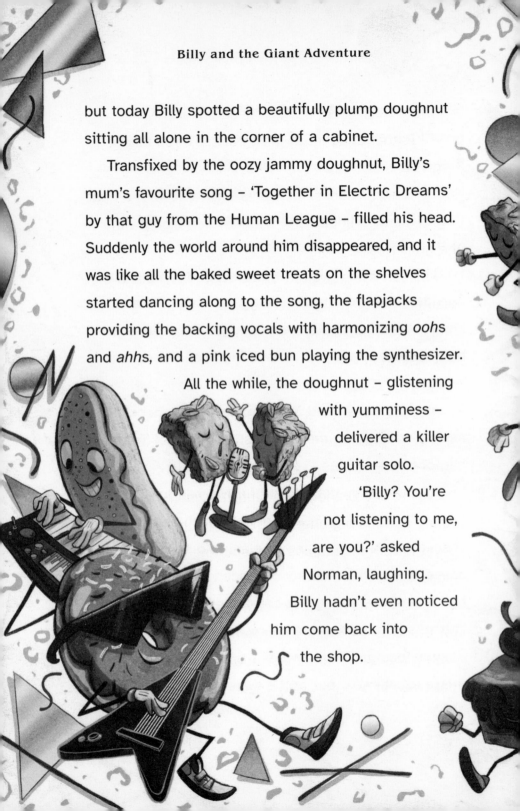

The bakery band in Billy's head fell silent.

'Is that doughnut winking at you? You take it – go on, son.'

'Really? Thanks, Mr Monk!' Billy said with a huge grin, as the shopkeeper bagged it up along with the groceries.

As soon as he got out of the shop, Billy raised the beautiful doughnut aloft, closed his eyes in anticipation, unable to wait even a second for that first satisfying bite.

SNATCH!

'Oi! What you got there?'

The doughnut had been grabbed clean out of Billy's hand. He opened his eyes to see Bruno Brace stuff the whole delicious thing into his big chops with a smirk, pushing it right in with his thumbs, jam spurting out all over his school tie.

Despite his earlier bravery, Billy was still scared of Bruno. But if there's one thing you didn't mess with it was Billy's food, and now Bruno had done that twice in one day. Billy knew that stealing wasn't right, and after everything that had happened today he could bottle it up no more.

So, as Bruno walked back towards his mob of ratty mates, Billy gathered up all his bravery and shouted: 'Hey, Bruno! That's two meals you owe me now – you're going to regret that!'

Bruno stopped and slowly turned to face him with thunder in his eyes.

Billy had a sinking feeling that this wasn't going to go well, but he also knew that Bruno wouldn't be able to reply yet. Billy himself had attempted to eat a whole doughnut once, and while the combo of soft, fluffy outer and squishy, jammy inner was perfect in a single mouthful, when you pushed a whole doughnut in at once it sucked all the moisture out of your entire body, leaving you unable to talk or function.

Bruno's crew started sniggering, gobsmacked that anyone would dare challenge their big-mouthed leader.

Bruno had no choice but to spit out the doughnut. Catching his breath, he stammered, 'D-don't you talk to me like that. Now you're gonna get it.'

Billy's heart felt like it was about to bounce out of his chest. His upper lip started to get sweaty, and his palms felt cold.

'Wait, Bruno. Let's . . . let's just talk it out?' he said.

But Bruno wasn't listening. Instead, he was making his way towards Billy, who, quick as a flash, grabbed his skateboard and got on the move, carving it up and gaining a good distance from Bruno and his mates.

He was almost far enough ahead to completely lose them when he nearly crashed straight into old Mrs Livings. She was struggling up the road, laden with shopping bags, and just managed to move out of the way of the oncoming Billy and avoid a full-on crash. But, as she swung her bags to the side, one of them split, sending fruit and veg rolling off in all directions.

'Oh, dear me,' she said.

Billy stopped in his tracks. He knew that this would mean Bruno and his mates would catch up with him, but he couldn't leave poor Mrs Livings to struggle in the road.

'Sorry, Mrs Livings!' he said, putting on his best smile and trying not to think about the fact that Bruno would be here any minute. 'Let me help you pick up your shopping.'

Billy got down on his hands and knees to round up all the scattered food. He was just grabbing the last plum when a shadow fell across him. He looked up to see a smirking Bruno.

'Oh dear, oh dear. You're in trouble now,' Bruno sneered. 'Grab him!'

Two of Bruno's bunch, the Jenkins twins, took Billy by the arms. Billy shut his eyes, bracing himself for the worst.

What a rotten day, he thought. *I wish I was safe and sound at Grandad's.*

Suddenly everything went quiet.

Really quiet.

Slowly Billy opened one eye.

Bruno's face hovered just in front of him, mid-sneer, while the Jenkins twins were like statues, still gripping Billy's arms. He glanced around. The birds in the sky were motionless, and even Mrs Livings was stuck with her mouth in mid-cry. It looked as if everyone had . . . frozen? Everything was silent, apart from Billy.

What the jammy doughnut is going on?! he thought.

Zzzzzwwwwwwoooooooooffff!

Billy jumped up at the newly familiar sound. Could it be . . . ?

'You's got yourself in a bit of troubles here, hasn't you, Mr Billy?' Basil said, flitting down on to his friend's shoulder. 'To be honest, I didn't expect you to be rubbin' that flint so soon. And I didn't expect I's able to come into your hooman land to see you. That's never happened before! This could get me in a lot of troubles, but it seems you and me we needs to help each other out. Looks like there's work to be done here, so let's crack on.'

Billy smiled with relief. He must have rubbed his flint necklace without thinking. Thank goodness his new friend had raced to help him!

'Now normally us Sprites likes to talk differences through to find a solution. That's the best way.'

'I know, Basil. My mum says that, too. But Bruno doesn't listen to anything I say. I've tried talking to him, but he just ignores me. At lunchtime, he threw a plate of food over my head, just to humiliate me in front of the whole school.'

'Hmmm,' said Basil. 'I thinks a little bit of good old-fashioned fun right back might puts a stop to it. I can't hold them like this for long, though. I's not really supposed to use magic in this way, so let's get started!'

Billy shunted Bruno into the position he'd just been in, right between the clutches of the Jenkins twins. Now for the rest of the crew. One by one, Billy quickly bent the boys' arms, sticking a finger up the next boy's nose like a giant nose-picking conga line. Then he tied all their shoelaces together.

Basil chuckled. 'That shoulds do the trick and give them a fright when I unfreezes them!'

'Wait!' said Billy.

He pulled his Polaroid camera out of his backpack, held it up and snapped a picture of the hilarious scene in front of him.

Basil nodded in approval. 'But I has one more little special finishin' touch to stop him running after you.'

And, with that, he undid Bruno's belt, whipping it out and wrapping it round his ankles.

'Right, Billy, ready to go? I needs to let this magic flow.'

Billy nodded, and Basil did a little jig in the air, then hid behind Billy's shoulder out of sight of the other humans, and the scene in front of them came back to life.

Bruno found himself being roughed up by the Jenkins twins. He grunted and shook them off in confused annoyance. The belt around his ankles caught him by surprise, and he tripped, his trousers falling down as he did so, stolen dinner money rattling across the pavement.

'Now, I didn't do that,' whispered Basil, pointing at Bruno's bare legs. 'Gravity's done that bit,' he said.

Bruno's pants were bright green with a red apple on the front and a worm coming out of it that said: THANK GOODNESS IT'S WEDNESDAY!

'Even us Sprites knows it's Friday today. Let's hope he's not been wearin' those pants for three days!' said Basil, his whole little body shaking with laughter.

The rest of the crew, realizing they were touching each other's bogeys, jumped back in horror and, in their hurry to disconnect the bogey conga, all tripped over their tied-up laces.

Bruno scrambled to his feet, and, at the same time, Mrs Livings noticed he had his trousers down, screamed and whacked him round the head with her handbag.

'Disgraceful behaviour,' she said, and scuttled away with her shopping, secretly giggling to herself. She winked at Billy as she passed.

Billy waved his Polaroid photo in the air. 'Maybe this will remind you to be kind, Bruno. Because, if anything happens to me or my friends, this picture might just end up on the front page of the local paper.'

'Great works, Billy,' said Basil, laughing. 'Now I's best be off home, before the chief notices I's where I shouldn't be!'

And *pop!* Off he zipped.

Smiling to himself, Billy quickly skateboarded away to deliver his grandad's shopping, ignoring the groans of Bruno and his crew who were still flailing about in utter chaos behind him.

When he got to Grandad's, Billy could tell his mum was already there because of the delicious smells wafting out of the kitchen.

'What's for dinner?' asked Billy, sitting down next to his grandad at the kitchen table.

'It's Friday, and that means it's a great day of the week for fish,' Grandad said with a smile. 'Your mum's got a lovely bit of plaice for us, and she's doing that thing that I love, aren't you, darling? She's an amazing cook, your mum.'

'Oh, Dad, it's nothing. Just a bit of chopped-up tomato, a few prawns, a dollop of cream, a sprinkle of cheese and a little pinch of the red stuff. What's it called?' She checked the tin. 'Oh yes, paprika.'

'It's not nothing. It makes an old man very happy.'

Mum served up the food with a spring in her step, and they all tucked in enthusiastically.

'Aren't we lucky?' Grandad smiled. 'Now what

adventures have you been having, Billy? I always love hearing about what you've been up to –'

He was interrupted by the orchestral sound of bins toppling over in the back garden, making him jump right out of his seat.

'Don't worry, Dad. I bet it's that pesky fox again.' Mum looked out of the back window. 'Yep, it's him all right. He's getting way too confident for my liking. Looks like he's scooping fish out of the stream. I'll go and chase him off.'

Billy waited for his mum to head out into the garden. He couldn't tell Grandad about the Sprites because he'd been sworn to secrecy, but he couldn't resist giving his ultimate best friend – his dear grandad – a hint of what had been happening.

'I've been going on lots of adventures, Grandad. *Real* adventures!' he whispered. 'Anna, Jimmy and me found a way to get into Waterfall Woods and –'

Grandad's face fell, stopping Billy in his tracks. 'Oh no, no. You don't want to be going in there, son,' he said. 'People in this village stay away from those woods for good reason.'

There was an uncomfortable silence. Billy had never experienced a feeling like this with his grandad before. Usually, he was really excited to hear all about Billy's escapades.

Grandad took a deep breath and put his knife and fork down, his eyes staring off into the distance.

'When I was a boy, about the same age as you are now, something terrible happened, and all these years later it's still a mystery.' He shuddered, and held up

his arm, where Billy could see that the little hairs were standing on end.

'Two boys, brothers, went into the woods, but only one of them came out. No one knew what had happened – just that one brother vanished into thin air and the other . . . Well, the other might have come home, but he was never the same. He lost an eye that day – he said he was attacked by a wild beast or something – but no one actually ever knew what happened to him or his brother.'

Billy gasped. No wonder people in the village avoided the woods!

'The whole village looked for the missing boy. I remember people coming from far and wide to help for months, but he was never found. It was a long time ago now, but even so Waterfall Woods has its secrets. Billy, you and your friends are best to stay away. Do you hear me? Stay. Away.' Grandad's fists were tightly clenched.

'OK, Grandad, I promise,' said Billy, but he crossed his fingers behind his back, feeling guilty about lying to Grandad as he did so.

Grandad's story didn't ring true about the woods Billy had come to know. The worst thing he'd encountered were the stinky Boonas, and Chief Mirren had said that they had only recently started being really mean.

It didn't make sense – Billy hoped that Basil might know what Grandad was talking about. And besides, even though he didn't like the sound of the wild beast in Grandad's story, Billy couldn't just abandon his new friends when he'd promised to help them.

Mum came back in from the garden, looking confused. 'There's a few dead fish in that stream, Dad, which is odd. The fox is having a field day. I've chased him off. To be honest, I'm not sure the fish looked good enough to eat! Anyway, the pub will be getting busy, so I'd better get back – you ready, Billy?'

'*Muuuuum*,' Billy said with a smile, 'could I stay here tonight, please? If that's OK with you, Grandad?'

He wasn't finished with his questions about Waterfall Woods just yet . . .

Grandad nodded, always pleased to have Billy's company, and so the deal was done.

As his mum got her things together, Billy quickly borrowed one of Grandad's envelopes, slipped the Polaroid photo of Bruno and his gang inside and handed it to his mum for safekeeping.

'Mum, if anything ever happens to me, like if I die, please can you make sure you give that to the local paper for me? It's really important.'

'You are a funny boy!' Mum said, slotting it into her

handbag. That was always her answer when Billy said something dramatic. 'Now be good for Grandad, and don't stay up too late. Oh, and make sure you brush your teeth before bed!' she shouted as she ran down the front path.

Billy and Grandad tidied up the kitchen and then squeezed up on one of the reclining chairs together – with a mug of hot chocolate for Billy and a hot toddy for Grandad – and Billy seized his chance to quiz him some more.

'Grandad, have you heard of something called the Rhythm?'

Grandad grinned. 'The *rhythm*? Oh yes!'

Billy was excited. He knew his grandad would be able to help!

'If your nana – God rest her soul – was here, she'd tell you all about the first time we met in the dance hall. I'm sure it's my hips and feet that got her attention. I used to dance ever so fast – you couldn't even see my legs move!'

'That sounds . . . great, Grandad. But I meant the Rhythm of nature?'

'Oh, the Rhythm of nature! Now that's something altogether different. My grandad used to talk to me about it. It's how everything's connected: we all have our place, and we all need each other.'

'That's right,' said Billy.

'It's like the ultimate version of teamwork and, sadly, I'd say we humans have probably started disconnecting from it. There used to be lots of small farms growing all kinds of different foods; now everything seems to be about big farms. Big ain't always best, Billy,' he said, tutting. 'We can be greedy and short-sighted. Everyone thinks you need to look to the future for answers, but I think sometimes the answers might just lie in the past. At one time, people worked in harmony with nature, but recently we seem to be trying to control it. Now, why are you worrying about it, young Billy?'

'Some friends told me about it, and how things don't feel quite . . . right at the moment,' said Billy. 'I want to help if I can.'

'Well, that sounds like a good thing to do. And I'm no expert, but maybe, if your mum's right about those

fish in my stream out there, then perhaps it's the water that needs looking at?'

Billy nodded. *Water*. That sounded like a good place to start.

'Now,' said Grandad, 'you've got three choices. Do you want to play Battleships, Guess Who? or watch *The Paul Daniels Magic Show*? I've heard he's going to try and saw his partner in half!'

'I've seen a lot of magic recently,' Billy said with a small smile. 'So Guess Who? it is then.'

'OK, Billy, but I can't promise not to beat you!'

Chapter 4

Battle of the Treehouse

The next morning, Billy woke up with a jolt. Bright-eyed and buzzing with energy, he jumped out of bed and ran downstairs. He found Grandad in the kitchen, stirring a pot of porridge.

'Ah, Billy, just in time. I want to let you into a very special and secret breakfast routine.'

Billy was intrigued. *What could it be?*

'I'm going to show you how to make perfect porridge. This will change your life forever – you mark my words, son!'

Billy raised an eyebrow. He wasn't sure that porridge could be life-changing, but he trusted his

grandad, and porridge was clearly no joking matter
for him.

'You need nice big rolled porridge oats, a little
pinch of salt, and water – never, *ever* milk. But don't
worry – we'll add that later. Put it all in a nice deep
pot, mix it with a wooden spoon, and let it simmer for,
oh, say . . . fifteen minutes. That will get it to the
perfect consistency.'

Billy's stomach rumbled. He wasn't sure he could
wait that long.

'Ha!' said his grandad, who'd obviously heard the
hunger pangs. 'Lucky for you, I've got a pot ready and
waiting, and this next bit is when the magic happens.
Here, put some of this hot, silky porridge into your
cold bowl – that creates a skin on the top *and* bottom.
Trust me.'

Billy did just as his grandad said.

'Sprinkle on some brown sugar –' Grandad shook
the sugar across the bowls with a flourish – 'and let it
sit for one and a half minutes *exactly*. I know, I know!
Be patient – it's worth it.'

Billy watched, and somehow the sugar seemed to

suck out all the moisture from the porridge, melting into what looked like an incredible golden syrup that trickled to the bottom of the bowl, magically releasing the porridge so it floated like an island in a syrupy sea.

'Wow, Grandad – look at that!' Billy's mouth was watering.

'You wait, son. I'm not done yet.'

Finally, Grandad showed Billy how to use a spoon and a knife to criss-cross the surface with four cuts each way.

'Add a drizzle of cold milk – and it's got to be full-fat gold-top – and here, watch,' Grandad said, pulling Billy close. 'Look how the milk creeps slowly into all the gullies. Bingo! You've got twenty-five perfect mouthfuls!'

Billy couldn't wait to tuck in, and he had to say it was the best porridge ever! He scoffed it all down with delight. Now that he'd learned the trick, Billy knew he'd never eat his porridge any other way.

Although he loved spending time with his grandad, Billy was itching to get home. Andy was *finally* back from his holiday, and they'd all agreed to meet at the treehouse that morning to debrief on everything that had happened while Andy had been away.

So, as soon as Billy had scraped his bowl clean, he gave Grandad a big loving hug goodbye and got going. Skateboarding away, not far from Grandad's house, he came across a fox lying by the side of the road. Living in the countryside, Billy was sadly used to seeing animals that had been hit by cars, but this felt different. He couldn't see any sign that the fox had been run over. It looked strangely beautiful and perfect . . . like it had just lain down and died.

He thought of the fox his mum had seen in Grandad's garden that had been eating the dead fish from the stream. What if this was the same one . . . ?

Maybe Grandad's on to something with the water, Billy thought.

When Billy got back to the pub, Anna, Jimmy and Andy were already in the treehouse, waiting for him, laughing their heads off. Andy was showing off a rather noticeable string-vest sunburn pattern all over the top half of his body – his main holiday feedback seemed to be that he had put on his mum's tanning oil, rather than the kids' suncream. And right now he was breakdancing and body-popping in an effort to show it in its best light.

There was no time for Andy to tell them anything else because the others couldn't wait to fill him in on their discoveries in Waterfall Woods. At first, Andy was sure that they were making it up. He'd fallen for a few of their tricks in the past. Jimmy had once done a triple whammy: not only had he convinced him they were long-lost brothers, he'd also spun a yarn about spaghetti growing on trees, and delivered a passionate speech about how honey came from bears. Another time, after a particularly big full moon, Billy had talked him into believing the moon was in fact made from cheese. And most recently (just after the four of them had been to the cinema to see *ET*) Andy had believed Anna's story of spotting an actual alien in their village. So today he took some convincing.

However, after listening to his friends talk about Sprites, Boonas and the magic of the woods, and coming up with a plan to solve the mystery of what had gone wrong with the Rhythm, Andy was pretty sure they were telling him the truth. It wasn't long before he was as keen as they were to help the Sprites uncover what had upset the balance of nature.

'I asked Grandad what he knew about the woods, and he told me a story about something that happened a long time ago. Apparently, a boy disappeared,' Billy told them. 'Grandad got really angry. I've never seen him like that before. He didn't want us to go back to the woods ever again.'

'So what should we do?' asked Jimmy.

'I told Chief Mirren that we'd help, so I think that's

what we should do. It sounds like the Sprites might run out of food. What happens if they can't find anything to eat? Or if the Boonas get worse? We can't let that happen because of a few old rumours! And a promise is a promise.'

'I'll go back if you do,' said Anna, and Jimmy nodded.

They all turned to look at Andy.

He shrugged. 'Course.'

'When I asked him about the Rhythm being off, Grandad said we should think about the water, so maybe that's where we should start,' Billy suggested.

They were interrupted by Billy's dad calling up to them. 'Come on, you lot! Parent approaching!'

The treehouse was at the very bottom of the garden, tucked away round a corner and well out of sight from the pub, but Billy's dad had trekked all the way there with a special delivery. The hatch door swung open, and his head popped up. He was in the middle of belting out the chorus of 'Livin' on a Prayer' by Bon Jovi.

Billy tried to shut the hatch door. 'Dad, you're

so embarrassing, and you know you're not allowed
in here.'

The singing continued, but Billy's dad winked and,
as his head disappeared down the hatch, his arm
came back up with a plate full of silky egg sandwiches,
with condiments galore.

'No way! Thanks, Dad!'

His dad disappeared back up the garden, but not
before shouting a warning to Andy to avoid too many
eggs.

'You're going to love these,' said Billy to his friends.
'Special silky omelette sandwiches – with an oozy
combo of Cheddar and Red Leicester cheeses and a
squirt of ketchup. So good. Well, like Dad said, maybe
not for you, Andy.'

'Um, I do have a confession to make,' Andy said
sheepishly. 'I had beans on toast for breakfast this
morning . . .'

Andy had a nickname – the Fart Blaster! And I bet
you can guess where that name came from. So,
knowing that he'd had beans already that morning,
and not wanting to risk a double-gas explosion, his

friends tried to make sure that Andy *didn't* take a sandwich, but he grabbed one anyway.

'Andy!' cried Jimmy. 'Not eggs *and* beans. You'd better keep your distance!'

Anna groaned and rolled her eyes, holding her nose and pulling a face. 'Guys, let's get going before Andy's bottom starts to burp.'

Refuelled and ready for action, the friends began gathering their stuff together to head off to the woods.

After an hour of critical planning, Billy suddenly felt the flint around his neck beginning to heat up. He quickly pulled it out from under his top. Was Basil in trouble again?

It got hotter as a message seemed to etch itself slowly into the stone:

TROUBLE'S COMING!

'Hey –' Billy started to say to his friends, but before he could finish there was a familiar high-pitched zooming noise. An instant later, Basil was on his shoulder.

'Oh, Billy, I think yous alls is in real danger, and it's my fault,' Basil said, rushing to get his words out.

Andy let out a cry as he came face to face with his first-ever Sprite! Anna quickly put her hand over his mouth.

'The reason we's not supposed to leave the woods is that we risks other beings leavin' the woods as well,' Basil said, looking guilty.

Andy shrugged himself free of Anna.

'IS THAT THE FAIRY?' he shouted, jumping up

and down. This time it was Billy's hand that covered Andy's mouth.

'I's not a fairy. I's a Sprite. *Fairies is mythical – we is magical!* Whys do you hoomans always think that I's a fairy?' Basil snapped at Andy. 'Anyways, this mornin' I sees these Boonas searchin' round the woods, and I hears them talkin' about hoomans and gettin' their own back . . . I thinks they's on their way to find you, Billy!'

'I can't believe it!' Andy said, still jumping up and down. 'A Sprite! Right in front of me!'

'Andy, calm down,' Jimmy said. 'Remember what happens when you –'

Right on cue, a loud fart slipped out of Andy's bottom with considerable force.

'Andy!' they all cried.

He rubbed his gurgling belly and shrugged. He was used to it, but today it was particularly gurgly.

'Goodness me!' Basil cried, pinching his nose. 'You best be careful where you points. You'll do someone real damage.'

'Everyone be quiet,' said Anna. 'This is serious, Billy. Seriously serious.'

'She's right. It's serious. Boonas might be many things, but they has good noses,' Basil said. 'And they be trackin' you, I's sures of it – they got a piece of your clothes. I recognized the colour.'

'My T-shirt!' Billy cried, remembering that one of the Boonas had ripped it when he was last in the woods. 'They must be SO angry with me for saving Basil the other day. I bet they want to get their own back. These Boonas are tough, guys! We need to be prepared.'

A **crash** came from outside, and a big dent appeared in one of the panels on the side of the treehouse. The air was filled with the sound of knocking and angry cries.

The gang peered nervously out of the window. Billy had been expecting to see the Stinker clan he'd beaten in the woods, but there were loads more Boonas than that. At least twenty or twenty-five creatures were heading into his back garden and throwing stones, mud and whatever else they could find on the ground at his treehouse!

'What do we do?' Jimmy said, wide-eyed.

Billy knew now wasn't the time to panic. He also knew that his parents weren't going to be of any use – they'd never hear them calling for help through the noisy chaos of a busy Saturday lunchtime in the pub. And, even if they *did* hear anything, they'd never in a million years believe it could be a Boona attack. Grown-ups just didn't seem to believe in stuff like that. Even things right before their own eyes! But Billy had defeated the Boonas once before, and this time he had the backup of his three best friends and Basil, not to mention his ambush-ready treehouse. He knew they could do this together.

'Right,' he said firmly, ducking to miss the stones that whizzed in through the window and smacked into the treehouse walls, 'let's show them what we're made of. Grab everything useful you can – this whole place is stocked with stuff. I was expecting to keep Bruno out, not hairy, angry Boonas, but maybe it's not that different!'

Everyone jumped into action, gathering catapults,

balls, marbles, sticks and random old tools that Billy
had nabbed from his parents' treasure-filled shed.
Then Billy quickly pulled up the ladder, knowing the
worst thing that could happen would be for a Boona
to get into the treehouse.

All the while, the Boonas were throwing more and
more rocks and bits of mud through the window and
started to gather underneath the treehouse.

'OK, we need to get rid of them before they try
to get in!' shouted Billy. 'Jimmy – you look after
the window. Anna – you cover the hatch. Take the
marbles and the catapult and get firing! Andy –
you back up whoever needs help the most! Basil –
keep a lookout for surprises. I'm going to distract
them.'

He ran over to the window. 'Hey!' he cried, leaning
out and looking down on the Boonas. 'Remember me?'

'That's the one!' they shouted. 'You're going to get
it, Skinny Bones!'

'If you want me, come and get me!' yelled Billy,
pointing to a fake ladder he'd set up underneath the

treehouse to fool anyone trying to get in without his permission.

But the Boonas didn't know that the ladder was a Billy-Boy Special! It was booby-trapped with broken steps and had hidden mousetraps, armed and ready to snap. And even if someone made it up the ladder, Billy had another trick up his sleeve. A fake door that was painted on, rather than actually leading into the treehouse.

The Boonas started queuing up at the bottom of the ladder. They scrambled up the steps, pushing and shoving each other. But the Boona at the front suddenly let out a wail as its hand landed on a mousetrap. Arms spiralling, it fell bottom first into the face of the Boona behind. Another one slapped its foot on a broken step, crashing downwards and causing a tidal wave of falling Boonas. They all collapsed on the ground in a stinky, sticky pile of arms, legs and bums.

Billy grinned, pleased with the pile-up. But there was no time to celebrate – more Boonas were

charging into the garden!

'What should we do next, Basil? Basil . . . ?'

Billy hurriedly looked around. Basil was nowhere to be seen. Where had he gone? But there was no time to think as some of the Boonas were now forming a ladder of their own, standing on each other's shoulders to reach the treehouse.

'Get that catapult ready, Anna!' Billy cried.

A Boona had got to the top of the ladder and made a hole in the fake door. It poked its head through and looked around.

Anna tried to kick it away, but the Boona took a big bite out of one of her brand-new trainers,

seemingly swallowing a chunk of her foot in the process.

'*NOOO!*' cried Billy.

But, rather than scream, Anna smiled, then relaxed her feet, letting all her toes pop out. 'They were too big for me anyway. Just a bit of breathing space for my feet!'

Billy grabbed the closest thing to hand, which just happened to be one of his dad's trusty old frying pans. He whacked it square on the Boona's forehead, with a *GOOOOONNNNGGG!*

The stinky thing fell head first from the treehouse to the ground, taking out a few of its mates as it tumbled down.

Billy heard a high-pitched **'HELP!'** and looked down to see Basil tied to his mum's picnic bench with some washing line. He was stuck fast. But Billy wouldn't be able to help just yet. They were all trying their best to keep the Boonas at bay, but it was clear they were outnumbered and running out of ideas to hold off their attackers!

Billy looked around. Surely there had to be something else they could use to get rid of these pests once and for all?

'*Ummmm* . . . Billy?' Andy's voice piped up.

'Not now, Andy! I'm thinking.'

'It's just . . . I'm not feeling too good,' Andy mumbled, rubbing his stomach.

Then it dawned on Billy. That was it! Andy *was* their greatest weapon. Andy's face reddened as grumbles and rumbles reverberated from his tummy.

'Anna, catch!' Billy cried, picking up a lighter and

throwing them to her. 'Andy's ready to blow . . . Get ready!'

'I don't think I can hold it in much longer!' yelled Andy, turning purple.

Anna grabbed a tea towel and wrapped it round her hand. She nodded at Billy, poised for action.

'On the count of three!' cried Billy. 'One . . . two . . .'

Anna lit the flame.

'Three!' yelled Billy. 'Release the beast, Andy!'

He moved Andy round so his bottom faced out of the window. Anna heroically thrust the lighter in front of Andy's bum with one hand and pulled her T-shirt up over her face with the other. Jimmy backed away and covered his face too, preparing for the worst.

Andy let out a trump, but the flame was only about a metre long.

'Andy, we need more!' shouted Billy. 'This is all we've got left!'

Andy clenched his hands and nodded – he knew this was his moment to shine.

The trump crescendoed into an absolute ripsnorter. It was immense!

The smell alone should have been enough to knock the Boonas off their feet, but as the epic fart met the lighter's flame a fireball whipped from the window towards the angry Boonas in the garden, singeing all their hairy little bodies. The Boonas closest to the treehouse, who had been holding Basil captive, turned in fear, running as fast as they could back the way they'd come.

Billy jumped down from the treehouse and rushed to free Basil.

'Well foughts,' Basil said, hugging Billy's nose.

'Billy,' wailed Andy from the treehouse window, 'I think there's another one coming . . . and this time it might be twins.'

Basil seized the moment to help his human friends. 'I suggest yous gets out of here, nasty Boonas!' he yelled at the few stragglers who hadn't yet run away. 'Yous don't want to be around for what happens next.'

The Boonas didn't need telling twice! Pushing and

shoving each other, they started to retreat.

'What was that weapon?' Billy heard one Boona say in awe. 'It was something we've never seen before. Such power . . .'

As the last Boona left the garden, Billy, Anna, Jimmy and Andy looked at each other, exhausted but victorious.

'False alarm,' Andy said with a shrug. 'I think it's all out now.'

'Well done, Andy!' whooped Anna. 'You saved the day!'

Basil settled on Billy's shoulder. 'Looks like you didn't need Sprite assistance today,' he said.

'That was actually really scary. How did they get out of the woods?' Jimmy asked.

'Now there's a question. Somethin's changed since yous came to see us. It's like Chief Mirren says to yous: things is gettin' worse with the Rhythm. I just hopes that those Boonas wasn't seen by any grown-up hoomans, because then we's havin' a big problem,' Basil said. 'I tells yous one thing: our worlds is not meant to collide. No offence, but yous hoomans is ruinin' your world. If yous lot gets a sniffs of ours, who knows what will happen?'

'We can come back to the woods and help you figure out what's going on,' offered Billy. 'If things have changed since we first met, it might be something we've done. I bet the solution is right under our noses. I promise we won't let you down.'

'*Biiiilllly!* Teeeeeatime!' yelled Mum from the pub. 'It's *ready*!'

Basil jumped at the sound of a grown-up's voice. 'Oh, I should be offs. Can't have your grown-ups seein' me either. But can I tell yous somethin'?'

'Of course,' Billy replied, intrigued.

'I found somethin' earlier,' he said. 'When the Boonas catched me, they locked me in that messy pantry for hours. I was flittin' around and I noticed a tiny little scroll in one of their piles – Boonas is hoarders, yous know – and it's so small they must have thought nothin' of it. I grabbed it just before they trapped me in that glass, but now that I's had a look I know it be a Sprites' map. And, if it's what I thinks it is, it's a very important, ancient Sprite map, and the most beautiful map I ever did see. It tells of a secret –'

'*Biiiillllly!*' Mum called again.

'No time – I needs to go! But comes to the woods as soon as you can, and I will tells you more!'

Defeating a troop of Boonas is very hungry work, you know. Luckily, Billy's mum had made them all a big pot of Billy Bolognese with spaghetti. The key to the best Bolognese in the whole wide world was taking the time to cook loads of finely chopped vegetables until golden and sticky, before browning the mince, adding a special selection of herbs, then tomatoes galore that she crushed into the mixture with her bare hands.

Billy's mum always left it blipping away, low and slow, for hours, creating the most incredible flavour. The final flourish was grated cheese on each portion, which was met with rounds of applause from the kids. Bowls of it were devoured and seconds too (plus sneaky thirds for everyone!). It was one of Billy's all-time favourite meals, which is why his mum had named it after him.

'Anyone got room for pudding?' Billy's mum asked, already knowing the answer. 'I have some marshmallows you can toast.'

As Billy and his friends twirled their marshmallows in the gas flames of the cooker, the puffy, soft sweets turned a gooey golden brown. Billy couldn't help but smile as it reminded him of the singed Boonas running away. A historic treehouse victory, and it was all thanks to their brilliant secret weapon – Andy the Fart Blaster.

'OK, I think it's time for sleep now – it's getting late!' I said with a yawn.

'Dad, no! You can't stop now!' cried Autumn. 'We need to know more about Basil's map. And they were just about to go back to Waterfall Woods for another adventure!'

'And I want to know more about Andy and his secret weapon,' Jesse said, letting one go with a wink. 'Is that the end of the Boonas?'

'Well, you'll just have to wait and see. It's time for lights out!'

'Billy's trouble at school with reading and writing sounds just like me,' Autumn said quietly.

'Exactly,' I said. 'And, just like you, he worked out a way to do things that was all his own.'

Autumn smiled.

'But now it's time for bed! We'll carry on tomorrow night. And remember: this is our secret story – twinky promise?'

I reached out my hand, stretching my little finger

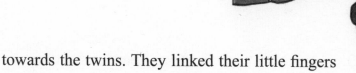

towards the twins. They linked their little fingers
with mine to confirm our pact.

The next night, a miracle happened. Both kids were
in their pyjamas, teeth brushed and lying tucked up
in bed without even having to be asked. Clearly, my
story had them hooked.

'Come on, Dad,' Autumn said. 'Time to get back
to the woods!'

'I thought you said that anything from the
eighties would be boring?' I said, ruffling her hair
with a smile.

'Yeah,' Jesse said. 'Please tell us what happens
next.'

'All right, cuddle in tight. Ready? Now, where
was I . . . ?

Chapter 5

The Lost City

It was Sunday and the weather had turned – it was wet, grey and howling a gale. Billy was woken up by rain pelting against the window and, blurry-eyed, he turned to check his alarm clock, letting out a groan when he realized he'd overslept.

The whole gang had promised to meet first thing to go back to the woods. They all wanted to help the Sprites uncover what was going on with the Rhythm and to find out more from Basil about his map. There was a lot to do, and they only had two days left of the long weekend. And now Billy was going to make them late!

He'd been unable to sleep because of all the excitement of the day – and thinking ahead in case the Boonas came back, Billy had spent the evening cutting, glueing, soldering and preparing tools for any future Boona (or Bruno!) attacks.

The one thing he was regretting was that he'd used his alarm clock for parts, meaning it hadn't gone off that morning!

There was no time to waste. He needed to get up, but Billy's thoughts were interrupted by the delicious smell of sausages wafting up to his room.

With bangers on the menu, his dad had to be on breakfast duty, and because of Dad's Special Sizzle Moment Billy knew they'd be extra delicious . . .

Surely the others won't mind me having a sausage sarnie to get the day started? Billy thought. *Even if it does mean I'm a little late . . .*

He entered the kitchen to see his mum reading the newspaper at the table while his dad hummed happily at the stove, stirring a pan full of sausages. Billy jumped on to a chair to watch the master at work.

'You ready, Billy?' asked Dad with a wink. 'Here comes the sizzle!'

He grabbed a bottle of Worcestershire sauce from the worktop, then, just as the sausages turned the perfect shade of golden brown, he began to furiously shake the bottle over the pan. The sausages spat and sizzled, wriggling around as if they were excited about the delicious meal being created. It was always quite a sight to behold, but today Dad was making even more of a performance of it as he sang along to Otis Redding's 'Sittin' on the Dock of the Bay', dancing in his dressing gown and slippers.

'Pass us the *hoooooooney*, honey,' he chorused.

Mum sprang across the kitchen and spooned a little runny honey into the pan, creating the ultimate sticky fat sausage, primed and ready for a soft, spongy bap.

But Dad wasn't done yet! He opened the window and held the pan out in the chilly air for thirty seconds – all the while performing some extra-special dance kicks that gave Billy and Mum a right giggle. It was just long enough to let the air cool down the outside of the sausages, solidifying the honey and making them nice and sticky. Totally weird, but totally worth it.

'You know what? I think your dad's Special Sausage Sarnie could fix anything in life,' said Mum, dropping her paper to pick up one of the baps.

Billy was just reaching out to grab his when he heard the crackle of his walkie-talkie coming from upstairs. He picked up his sandwich and got up, ready to run to his room . . .

'Um, where do you think you're off to?' asked Dad. 'Breakfast together at the table, please.'

'But, Dad, my walkie-talkie is going off!'

'Breakfast first,' Dad said firmly.

Billy sat down and practically inhaled his sausage sarnie in three giant, wonderfully satisfying mouthfuls, sticky glaze dripping down his chin.

'Finished!' he cried, jumping up triumphantly.

Dad laughed. 'That's my boy,' he said, shaking his head as Billy raced up the stairs.

'Beefburger One! Any breakers, any takers? This is Sassy Cat looking for a copy. Over.' *Tscccchhhhh.* Anna's voice came through loud and clear. **'Where is everyone?! Over.'**

'Roger that. This is Beefburger One receiving. Over!' replied Billy.

'Copy that. Thunderbug receiving. Over,' chimed in Jimmy.

'Pie here,' replied Andy.

'You have to say "over" at the end. Over,' said Jimmy.

'I thought my name was Pie?' came Andy's confused reply.

'It *is* Pie. It's not your name though; it's your *handle*, and you still have to say "over". It's like a full stop! Over,' replied Jimmy.

'**Anyway,**' said Billy, interrupting, '**I'm so sorry I overslept! I know we need to get going, but the weather really isn't on our side. Over.**'

'**Copy that,**' replied Anna. '**I'm ready and waiting. Hurry up! I've borrowed my brother's ski goggles. The rain won't be stopping me. Over.**'

'**Copy that. Great idea, Sassy Cat,**' said Billy. '**We'll meet at yours in ten minutes, yeah? Over.**'
Tscccchhhhh.

'**Gotcha. See you soon, Beefburger One. Over and out,**' replied Anna as they all signed off.

'Andy, what on earth are you wearing?' Anna asked as the friends gathered outside her house.

Andy looked down at his get-up and shrugged. 'My last waterproofs kind of melted,' he said.

'How?' said Jimmy.

'Don't ask,' he replied, pulling a face and pointing at his bottom. Everyone laughed. But there was no doubt Andy had been resourceful – he was wearing a large black bin bag with holes for his head and arms, held tight by one of his mum's belts so that it kicked out like a dress. It was something to behold, but as a waterproof layer it seemed to be working a treat, and Andy didn't care what he looked like as long as he was warm and dry.

'Right, let's go!' shouted Billy, and the friends headed for Waterfall Woods, whizzing down the hill and going full pelt through massive puddles.

As they drew closer to Wilfred Revel's cottage, they spotted the old man perched at his front gate, wearing a waxed jacket and a hunter's hat. Instinctively, they got off their bikes to walk past, not wanting to get into trouble.

'Morning,' muttered Mr Revel as they passed. 'Don't you go hanging around those woods. I've been told there's kids on bikes sniffing around, and, if it's you, stay away, you hear? It's not safe.'

'OK, Mr Revel – it's not us,' Billy replied nervously, fingers crossed behind his back. The others gave small polite smiles.

'My mum always used to say, people can lie with their words, but not their eyes.' Mr Revel pointed at them as they moved past him. 'I see you.' He lifted his eye patch, which they'd never seen him do before, and they gasped before scarpering. 'You'd better be careful,' he shouted after them.

Disturbed but undeterred, they got back on their bikes and sped off once more until they drew to a halt at the fallen elm tree. Stashing their bikes in the ditch, they looked around to make sure the coast was clear before using the branch to catapult their way over the big wall into the wood.

Billy, Anna and Jimmy led the way to the old oak tree with Andy trailing behind, wide-eyed as he took in the surroundings for the first time.

'WOW!' he said.

'See, we told you!' said Jimmy. 'It's pretty great, right? And this tree is ANCIENT!'

They carried on past the oak tree and towards the Sprites' village.

'Hang on a minute,' said Anna. 'How come it's so sunny all of a sudden?'

'You're right – the ground isn't even wet,' replied Jimmy, looking up at the sky in wonder.

'Who cares!' cried Andy, ripping off his outfit. 'At least now I can get out of this old bin bag!'

'Come on,' Billy said. 'Let's go and find Basil.'

They walked further into the woods and soon reached the Sprites' dwellings. Something definitely wasn't right – at this time of year, approaching the peak of summer, new life and colour should be bursting everywhere, but this looked more like an autumn scene. Leaves were starting to drop, and everything felt a bit grey, brown and sad. There were lots of Sprites buzzing around, but no sign of Basil.

Billy's heart skipped a beat. Basil had known they were coming this morning, so why wasn't he here to

greet them? What if he'd been captured by the awful Boonas again? They'd be even keener for revenge after yesterday! Billy was flooded with guilt – were all these things partly his fault?

'Excuse me,' he said politely to a passing Sprite. 'Where's Basil?'

'We's a bit worried actually,' the Sprite replied. 'We thinks we's lost him.'

'*Lost* him?' Anna asked.

Another Sprite whizzed forward. 'I's Myrtle. Basil was talkin' last night about goin' into the deep, dark parts of the woods –'

'Where we is absolutely forbidden to go,' interjected another Sprite.

'Sage is right,' Myrtle agreed, nodding at the other Sprite. 'Chief Mirren says we is not allowed in those dangerous parts of the woods. Basil's in a whole lot of trouble.'

'He told everyone that he found an old map showin' the ways to an ancient Sprite city called Balthazar,' Sage said. 'He was right rabbitin' on about it. Said he got the map when he was captured by the Boonas, and that we should go there for safety because of the Rhythm being offbeat. He said the Boonas had even found their way into your hooman land?'

'That's true,' said Jimmy. 'We saw them off yesterday!'

'I heard Basil arguin' with the chief and the other Elders,' Myrtle added. 'One of them said there might be somethin's in it, but most thoughts it be a trap set by the Boonas. That they wanted Basil to find the map. No one believed Balthazar could be real.'

'So you think Basil went off on his own to find it?' asked Billy.

This had to be the map he was talking about yesterday, but why wouldn't he have waited for Billy and his friends?

'Yes,' replied Sage. 'Basil usually follows the rules, but since he's met yous hoomans he's changed.'

'Some of us thinks yous might be bringin' a bit of bad luck to us Sprites,' said Myrtle sheepishly. 'Especially with all the changes to the Rhythm.'

By this point, lots more Sprites had gathered round to listen, all chattering away and clearly curious as to what was going on. But suddenly a hush fell over the clearing and the wall of Sprites parted. Chief Mirren flew through the crowd, stopping gracefully in front of the four friends.

'Hello, humans. As you've heard, once again we need your help. Basil should not have gone off by himself. It's very dangerous in the woods for a lone Sprite. Especially at a time when we know the Rhythm isn't behaving as it should,' Chief Mirren said, frowning. 'Basil told us that the Boonas had entered your world. Things are not as they're meant to be, and we must fix whatever has happened before it's too late. But, right now, I am worried about Basil's safety.'

In the back of Billy's mind, he couldn't help but think that maybe the Sprites, who were wary of humans, were right. Maybe it would have been better if he hadn't made the others explore the woods in the first place. Why did he always push his luck and mess things up? Well, if he had caused this and Basil was in danger, then he had no choice but to put things right.

'We can find him,' Billy told the chief bravely. His friends nodded furiously in agreement.

'I wish we had taken this map more seriously when he mentioned it,' the chief said. 'But there is so much more to do. Luckily, I had a feeling Basil might decide to take matters into his own hands, so before he left my parlour I decided to tag him just in case.'

'Oh no!' said Andy, thinking of his Uncle Kev's new electronic prison tag.

'Please don't worry,' said Chief Mirren. She opened a little box of luminous orange dust. 'This is crushed saffron. We use it in celebration meals, but it's also useful for tracking things. I popped some under Basil's wings – it should leave a trail of little specks throughout the woods, and, if you can't see it, you should be able to smell it when the sun heats it up.'

There was a little rustle, and a violet-blue Sprite called Rosemary flew forward confidently, dragging another smaller Sprite with her.

'Chief Mirren!' said Rosemary, her big bright eyes glinting with excitement. 'Cassia and I would both like to help the hoomans.'

'Would we?' asked Cassia, who clearly hadn't signed up for this. Her cute button nose flared in confusion, causing her ears to twitch.

Rosemary nudged her to be quiet. 'With my pin-sharp eyesight and Cassia's brilliant sense of smell, our senses is superior to theirs – and you know we's your best trackers.'

'Yes, we is,' agreed Cassia proudly, warming to the idea now.

Chief Mirren looked unsure. 'There's a reason that Sprites aren't supposed to travel beyond our village boundary. I'm not sure I can put more Sprites in danger just because of Basil's recklessness,' she said.

'But there's four hoomans to protect us,' Rosemary said. 'We'll be very careful.'

'We'll take good care of them, I promise,' Billy said, hoping to help their cause. It sounded like they could use both Sprites' extraordinary tracking skills to find Basil.

Chief Mirren hesitated, then said, 'All right, I will grant permission this once because we all want Basil to return home safely.' She turned to Billy. 'Rosemary and Cassia will be most helpful to you, I'm sure. But I'm trusting you to keep them safe.'

Rosemary took the lead. She seemed to have already seen something that was way beyond the view of the others. She stopped and pointed to a tree in the distance. 'There's saffron on its bark.'

Billy slipped his backpack hood over his head and adjusted the focus of his mini binoculars with the hood strings. 'Wow! You really have got amazing eyesight,' he said, pleased they were on the right track.

'We should go as quickly as possible to catch up with Basil,' Jimmy suggested. 'He's bound to be taking his time to study the map carefully. If we run, we have a better chance of finding him.'

'Good idea,' said Anna. 'Rosemary, you carry on taking the lead and follow the saffron specks!'

They set off again at a faster pace, the kids running while the Sprites whizzed through the air above them. They were now deep into the woods and, as they turned into a clearing, the Sprites suddenly came to a stop.

'What's the matter?' asked Billy.

Cassia and Rosemary looked uncomfortable.

'Boonas!' whispered Rosemary. Cassia nodded, holding her nose.

And, sure enough, as the little party quietly edged their way forward, they could see a huddle of Boonas ahead. They were busy making traps for wild animals – and unsuspecting Sprites – and didn't notice the group approaching them.

Carefully, they skirted past the Boonas, everyone holding their breath to avoid inhaling too much of the dreadful stench coming from the creatures.

The good thing about the awful stink was that as the air began to smell fresh and clean again they knew they must be clear of the Boonas' territory.

'Phew!' sighed Billy, taking a big deep breath. 'I'm glad to be away from them.'

They continued on and soon reached a stream, which meandered and eventually widened into a river.

'Hey, look,' said Jimmy, pointing to the riverbank.

All along the side of the water, the reeds, buttercups and plants looked sad and discoloured, as if they'd been burned by something.

'That's weird,' said Anna.

'We's noticed some plants is dyin' near our village, too,' said Cassia. 'But we doesn't know what's causin' it. We's never seen anythin' like it before.'

'It *is* really weird,' said Jimmy. 'When we're near the water, everything seems to be dead quiet. Something's not happy here.'

Billy looked at the stream. If this water linked to the stream in the village, then maybe the human world and the Sprite world were more connected than they realized . . .

'The trail continues over there,' Rosemary said, shaking Billy from his thoughts. She pointed to a row of rocks across the river that had flecks of orange on them.

'Let's keep going,' he said. They could only deal with one problem at a time. The water and the Rhythm would have to wait; for now, Basil was the one who needed their help the most.

'Where next, Rosemary?' asked Anna once they'd all crossed to the opposite bank.

Rosemary flitted around, looking confused. 'The saffron shows Basil goin' that way, then backtrackin' to here, then over there and under here,' she said, flying about in all directions.

'If I was him . . .' said Billy, 'I'd follow that trail,' and he pointed to the bottom of a mountain path.

'Yes.' Jimmy smiled. 'Remember – always follow the path of least resistance.'

Cassia sniffed the air. 'I think you's right. The saffron scent seems to be stronger in that direction.'

They started climbing. The path may have been well trodden by wild animals, but it was definitely not easy-going. The Sprites could zip on quite effortlessly, but it was a bit of a struggle for the others.

Andy looked up, shaking his head. 'First Sprites, then Boonas, now I'm climbing a flippin' mountain that seems to have popped up right next to our sleepy little village. Whatever next? Giants? Flying monkeys? The Wicked Witch of the West?'

As they got higher up the path, they had a spectacular view of the woods below. But Billy was confused that their village was nowhere to be seen – no pub, no school, no houses. It was like they were in a whole different world. One untouched by humans.

'It's so beautiful here,' said Anna, looking at the luscious green landscape around them.

'It's like we're in a different world,' Andy said, echoing Billy's thoughts. 'It's as if everything changed when we got into the woods.'

'But something's not quite right,' Jimmy replied softly, pointing to the network of streams and rivers.

Just like the one they'd come across in the woods, there were areas of burnt and bleached plants dotted around the streams and waterways beyond.

'Jimmy, I'm sure it's got something to do with the water. My grandad had loads of dead fish in the stream by his house. What do you think is going on?' asked Billy.

'I'm not sure,' Jimmy replied, 'but once we find Basil, we really have to look into it quickly.'

By now, they were near the top of the mountain, and the saffron tracks they'd been following suddenly stopped at a rock face.

'Where to next?' asked Jimmy. 'It looks like Basil's completely disappeared . . .'

Cassia started to move methodically over the surface of the rock, sniffing and snuffling as she went.

'Here!' she cried. 'There's a hole.'

They all crowded round.

'Basil must have gone through there, but it's way too small for us,' said Billy. 'Quick, everyone, start clearing the ivy to see if we can make it bigger.'

The friends began pulling at the leaves smothering the rock, gradually revealing a bigger entrance to a tunnel.

'Catch!' shouted Billy, tossing Anna a torch from

his backpack, while he flipped his hood on, pulling a cord to activate a light.

One after the other, with Billy leading the way, they climbed into the tunnel and started crawling along. With the torch lighting their path, it didn't seem too scary, despite the bits of rock jutting out. After a short while, it began to feel as if the space was opening up. They continued walking, until they came to a dead end.

'What do we do now?' asked Andy.

They looked around, hoping for a clue. Then Anna noticed a little shell, the pearly inside glinting in her torchlight.

'What's that doing here?' she wondered. 'We're nowhere near the sea.'

Rosemary fluttered up to Anna and gently put her tiny hand inside the shell. She pushed and twisted until the shell became one with the wall.

'Shells are often used as keys,' she explained. 'We Sprites uses them to open important rooms.'

The tunnel filled with the sound of whirring cogs, and Billy and the others gasped as the rock at the end of the tunnel rotated. Suddenly everything began to glow as beams of golden light streamed through from the other side of the wall along with a warm, sweetly scented breeze.

Everyone's eyes popped, and their mouths dropped in awe at the enchanting sight. They found themselves gazing out on a beautiful valley. It looked like it might be an old volcano, as jets of steam puffed out of the earth and the ground glowed, making the valley feel like a golden cup. There were all kinds of trees laden with fruit, brightly coloured butterflies fluttering in the breeze and melodic birdsong drifting in the air. There were also flowers of all sizes, from carpets of the teeniest most beautiful blooms to ones big enough for the kids to climb inside. In the near distance was a handful of buildings, some small, some huge. Right in the middle, forged out of the volcanic rock, was an incredible castle, with soaring walls that seemed to be carved out of the mountain itself. Alongside it, a cascading waterfall shimmered in the sunlight, making rainbows in the mist. It was a truly magical place.

'Balthazar!' Rosemary whispered in wonder.

'It's real,' said Cassia, smiling. 'The tales is true.'

'Look, a waterfall!' said Jimmy. 'That must be why it's called Waterfall Woods. It's all weirdly making sense now!'

'I sees saffron sprinkles again – Basil's definitely here,' said Rosemary. She pointed to the small orange specks. 'Look! Over there, up there, down here and under there.'

'How is we goin' to find him in such a massive place?' asked Cassia.

'*BAAAASSSSSSIIIIIIILLLLLL?*' Andy shouted at the top of his lungs.

'That'll do it,' said Billy, laughing. And sure enough, a moment later, Basil landed on Billy's shoulder.

'Basil! I'm so glad you're OK!' Billy said.

'OK? I is better than OK! I's wonderful. I knew the map I'd found was important, and I was right.' And, with that, Basil did a little celebration dance, finishing with the splits.

'But why didn't you wait for us?' asked Jimmy. 'We promised we'd come and help you.'

'Well, I waited, but after a while I thought yous

wasn't comin', so I decided to head out alone.'

Billy's stomach dropped. 'That was my fault, Basil. I'm so sorry!' he said. 'I overslept and held us all up.' Guilt flooded him again.

'Don't yous worries, Billy. I knows Chief Mirren and the other Elders wanted me to stay put, but I has to follow this heart of mine, even if it means goin' it alone. And look! It led me to this incredible discovery,' he said, beaming at Billy and the others.

'This be our true home that legends speaks of. And, what with all the strange happenin's that's been goin' on, Balthazar might have made itself known just when we alls needs it most . . . Wait a minutes – what's yous all doin' here? How did yous finds me?'

'You were tagged, mate,' Andy chipped in. He reached out and gave Basil a little nudge, causing more saffron specks to waft to the ground.

'I thought I smells a bit funny today . . . But never mind how yous found me. Come on – there's so much I's got to show yous alls!'

Basil zipped off, urging them to follow. It was then that Billy realized there was a moat just ahead, separating the mountain from the castle.

'I pressed that to open the drawbridge across,'
Basil explained, pointing to a small shell in a rock by
the bridge. 'I thinks this moat is to stop Boonas from
gettin' into Balthazar. It's too big to jump across.'

Everyone ran excitedly over the bridge and into a
charming courtyard in front of the castle. It looked like
some parts of the majestic towers were formed by
natural volcanic rock, and others had been sculpted
by hand.

Inside, the castle looked run down and in need of
a good clean, but even through the dust and debris
they could see what a brilliantly grand building it was.

Pretty, ornate floor tiles drew their eyes to
sweeping staircases that, in turn, led to vast opulent
rooms full of beautifully carved wooden chandeliers,
embellished with the sparkliest seashells, hanging
from iron chains.

'I don't think anyone's been here for absolutely
ages,' said Billy in awe.

'I reckon hundreds of years at least,' added Jimmy.
'But all the natural stuff is still in mint condition. Look

at the fountains and the pools. You can see the water springs connecting them. We could probably swim from one pool to another.'

'But why would anyone leave this place?' asked Anna. 'It's so beautiful.'

As they looked up, they could see stunning bedrooms dotted round the first-floor balcony, and an amphitheatre-like room off the central hall. They walked into a large room with lots of different-sized furniture, both huge and Sprite-sized, built into the walls.

'Why's that all so big if it's meant for Sprites?' Andy said.

Billy pointed to a massive flint plaque cut high into the wall with large etched words that read:

NO MATTER HOW BIG OR HOW SMALL,
THIS PLACE IS HOME FOR ALL.

'What do you think that means?' asked Anna.

'Look – there's one here, too,' said Basil.

Sure enough, below the plaque the words were repeated on a second sign, but this time super small, the lettering the perfect size for Sprites to read.

They frowned at each other, confused.

'Where's Andy gone?' Jimmy said, looking around.

His question was answered by an almighty scream from another room. They ran towards the sound and found Andy standing in a big hall.

'I j-just opened this door to have a look inside,' he stammered, pointing upward. 'Look!'

In the light-flooded room, the group followed Andy's gaze. Billy saw at once that this must have been a grand banqueting hall because there, right in the middle, was a giant table that soared up towards the high ceiling. The table was still laden with plates and goblets and even the remains of some long-ago feast. Slumped at the table were huge dusty skeletons.

'What . . . happened here?' asked Billy. 'And why are they so big? I thought this was an ancient Sprite city. These look like . . . Giants!'

'I reckon that they were just sitting down to a banquet, then were somehow poisoned. See, there's a skeleton over

there still holding a knife and fork,' Jimmy replied.

'There's always been tales of Giants, just like there's always been tales of Balthazar, but I never thought them to be true. But now . . . I doesn't know,' said Basil, flitting up to take a closer look at the enormous skeletons.

'In legends, Sprites and Giants were best friends, helpin' each others. But no livin' Sprite, not even the Elders, has ever seen a Giant, so we thought they was only stories,' Rosemary added.

'Something bad must have happened here,' Anna said. 'Maybe that's why Balthazar has been abandoned and forgotten for so long?'

'I guesses the Sprites fled to safety – I supposes it's much easier for little Sprites to escape than big Giants,' said Basil, zooming back down to the group. 'Someone or somethin' didn't want us here . . .'

'The Sprite history we knows only goes back so far,' Basil continued. 'The Elders holds all the stories of our legends, but Chief Mirren is the oldest of us all, and even she can't remember ever livin' beyond our dwellin's. I thinks that whatever happened here caused us Sprites to flee, so the younglings could go to safety and the Elders faced whatever needed to be faced. Likely they's never got out, and we needed new Elders to hold our stories.'

Rosemary gasped.

Basil went on. 'Maybe the escaped Sprites was too scared to talk about what really happened in Balthazar. Which is why there's all these legends, but no real truths.'

'Sounds like there's a lot to discuss with the rest of the Sprites,' said Anna. 'If you're right, Basil, this opens up a whole new part of your history.'

'Do yous thinks the danger has passed?' asked Cassia nervously.

'Looking at those skeletons, whatever happened here took place a very long time ago,' said Billy. 'I'm sure we're safe. But, just to be certain, let's have a really good explore; then we can all go back to Chief Mirren and the other Sprites and tell them what we found.'

'Billy's right,' said Jimmy. 'We can look around the whole place and report back.'

'Yes,' added Anna. 'There's nothing to be afraid of
if we all stick together.'

'Nothing to be afraid of? You've just added twenty
dead Giants into the mix,' exclaimed Andy in disbelief.

But they were here now, and maybe Basil was right.
Perhaps Balthazar had *wanted* to be found. So they
set off to explore.

They discovered an old armoury, which Billy
thought was amazing – it was full of cannons,
cannonballs, catapults, spears and crossbows of all
sizes. There were also bottles of potions with labels
like ITCHING DUST, EXPLOSIVE POWDER and one saying DEADLY

POISON, complete with a skull and crossbones. There was even TAGGING POWDER, which was just like the saffron that Chief Mirren had used. And, by a huge door, there was a massive sword that nobody could move, let alone lift.

The same was true in other rooms: a mix of little and large, huge and small.

'I think there must have been a lot of respect between the Sprites and the Giants,' Anna said, looking at the platforms that ran along the edges of the walls. 'This place is built so that eye contact can be maintained at all times. It's been created for happy communication between the two groups.'

Before they set off back to the Sprite village, Billy used his Swiss army knife to help his friends pick amazingly ripe fruit from the trees and bushes.

They were blown away by what they tasted – the smallest bananas with the biggest flavour; a fruit that looked like a plum yet tasted more like bubblegum and changed to all the colours of the rainbow in the light. Then Basil showed them how to cut the bottom off an orange fruit and squeeze out some sort

of smoothie deliciousness. Even Andy, who thought he
hated fruit, tucked in with gusto.

He let out a little trump, which sounded like a
high-pitched whistle.

'Sorry, guys, blame all this fresh fruit,' he said, and
everyone rolled about giggling, apart from Cassia
who'd fainted.

'Now that we've had a good look around, and it
seems that any danger is long gone, we should get
going,' said Anna. 'All the Sprites were terribly
worried about you, Basil, and they'll want to know
you're safe.'

The group retraced their steps back down the
mountain path, across the river, up the stream, and
carefully through the Boona-infested woods, back to
the Sprite village. As they walked up the track, the
other Sprites saw them approaching and started to
line the path, clapping and cheering, like a fluttering
tunnel.

'Chief Mirren!' Basil cried, flying straight to her.
'I's sorry for goin' off on my own. I knows I's in
trouble. But the map really did lead somewhere

special – I needs to tell you and the other Elders alls about it!'

'Basil! I'm so relieved that you're safe,' Chief Mirren said with a smile. Then she looked serious. 'But you should not have gone alone. We'll discuss this later, as well as this special place you've found. But I'm sure our human friends should be returning home now as it's late in both our worlds.'

Billy nodded. 'Yes, we must get going. Please don't be too hard on Basil. He was just trying to do the right thing, even if it wasn't in quite the right way.'

Basil gave his friend a grateful smile.

'Before we go, we want to speak to you about the Rhythm, Chief Mirren,' said Billy. 'My grandad told me that when things go wrong in nature it's often the water. The plants on the banks of the river we crossed today looked awful, and we've noticed stuff like that in our world, too.'

'Water transcends all boundaries so, even though our worlds are separate, it could be possible that the problem with the Rhythm may be coming from your world. If this is the case, we would be powerless to fix it,' Chief Mirren said thoughtfully. 'I don't think you found us by accident – I believe the Myas have a plan and a purpose for you.'

'The Myas?' said Anna.

'The Myas *are* the woods,' Chief Mirren told them. 'They're the infinite and ever-regenerating colony of mycelium.'

'Mycelium – that's to do with fungi, isn't it?' Jimmy said.

'Yes, Jimmy,' said Chief Mirren. 'The Myas, like fungi, are not one but all. They're interconnected. They exist to assist, protect and balance the Rhythm. As things wither and die, the Myas generate new beginnings, ensuring the circle of life is everlasting.'

Billy, Anna and Andy looked confused.

'Think mushrooms,' Jimmy said to them. 'There's loads of them – on the ground, under the ground, even on your skin, everywhere you can think of. They break things down and clean things up. But they also feed things and create new life. Some people say they can communicate with each other. It sounds like the

Myas are very similar.'

'I think the Myas opened up our world to you, because you're the ones who can help restore the Rhythm and stop this dangerous path we're on,' said Chief Mirren.

The friends looked at each other in disbelief, their minds blown – there was so much to discover about this magical world.

'Leave it to us, Chief Mirren. We'll do everything we can to help, won't we?' said Billy.

Anna, Jimmy and Andy all chimed in with an enthusiastic 'Yes!' If the human world was causing damage to Waterfall Woods and the Sprites' land, they would do everything they could to put that right.

Back at the pub, Billy and the others found his mum in full swing, setting up for dinner service.

'Hello, love!' she yelled as she bustled round the tables. 'You lot hungry? We've got a lovely special on tonight – another of your favourites, Billy: rainbow-veg lasagne.'

'Yes!' cried Billy, punching the air and doing a little jig.

This was possibly the most bonkers lasagne ever made, but, boy, was it good. Layer upon layer of different-coloured veggies and pasta smothered with oozy, melty cheese, creamy white sauce, sweet tomato sauce, soggy bits and crispy bits – delicious! Billy had often seen even the most hardened meat-eaters devour a whole plateful.

Billy and his friends settled down in the kitchen, and as they tucked in – with bonus garlic bread on the side – they discussed everything that had happened that day and what they would do next.

Thank goodness it was a bank holiday weekend. That gave them tomorrow to do some investigating. If water really was the problem, they needed to head upstream and see what they could find . . . before things in the woods got even worse.

Chapter 6

Who's Wrecking the Rhythm?

'**W**ake up! Time for your morning shower, Billy!'
A sprinkle of water rained in through
Billy's bedroom window, and he woke with a start.
It was the beginning of his dad's bank-holiday ritual
– he'd lean all the outdoor furniture against the pub,
have a good sweep up and hose it all down, also
watering the beautiful flowers that adorned the front
of the old building. He was hoping that one day he'd
win the 'Best-Dressed Pub' award.

Dad had the loudest whistle on Planet Earth, and
his whistling ranged from Pet Shop Boys to Pavarotti.
While Billy could protect his ears with a pillow over

his head, he couldn't escape a soaking from the hose.

But for once Billy was happy with the wet wake-up call, as there was some serious work to be done.

He quickly got dressed and grabbed his walkie-talkie to let the others know he was on his way.

'This is Beefburger One ready for action. Over.'

The walkie-talkie crackled into life and his three friends replied, agreeing to meet at Jimmy's. They were ready to go! Billy grabbed his stuff and bounded downstairs.

'Someone's in a hurry!' his mum said with a laugh, as he flew towards the front door.

'I'm meeting the others!' Billy yelled, already halfway down the front path. 'We're on a mission!'

'All right, pet,' his mum said, clearly not really listening. 'Have fun.'

Billy jumped on his BMX and pedalled as fast as he could, keen to get started. For once, he wasn't worried as he approached Bruno's house. Even if Billy didn't have photographic evidence to rely on, when you've fought off Boonas and discovered hidden cities, the school bully doesn't seem such a big deal any more. In fact, spotting Bruno in his front garden, Billy even gave him a wave as he wheelied past his house.

'Morning, Bruno!' he cried, enjoying the shocked look on his rival's face.

He carried on down the hill – not forgetting a few tricks to make use of all the kerbs and bumps in the road – to Jimmy's, where he found Anna and Andy already waiting. Jimmy appeared from the back garden, looking like a clown as he wobbled along, having 'borrowed' his little sister's glittery lilac bike.

He then crashed clumsily, toppling off, but he simply brushed himself down and got back on. Without missing a beat, he pointed at the stream that ran alongside his house and said, 'Everything points to water being the thing that's affecting the Rhythm, so let's follow it upstream.'

They cycled along the little path beside the stream. It wasn't long before they began to notice sad-looking plants and little burnt and bleached areas of riverbank like they'd seen in the woods.

Suddenly Jimmy skidded to a halt and jumped off his bike.

'Oh no,' he whispered, kneeling down by the edge of the stream.

'What is it?' asked Anna.

Jimmy leaned over the water and used both hands to lift out a huge limp fish. It was a beautiful golden and olive-green colour, and its pretty scales shimmered in the sunlight. But there was no doubt that the fish was dead.

Jimmy looked like he might cry. 'The poor thing. What could have happened to it?'

'It has to be linked to what we've seen in the
woods. This proves it must be something in the water,
doesn't it?' said Billy.

'I think this pike might have been a breeding
mother,' said Jimmy. 'Which means that she could
have made hundreds of babies – this is really bad.'

'What should we do with it?' Anna asked. 'I don't
think it's a good idea to put it back in the water.
It might contaminate it even more.'

Billy nodded. 'I think you're right. We should bury
it instead.'

Jimmy gently placed the fish in the undergrowth,
and his friends helped him cover it with leaves and soil.

'I hope we don't find any more of those,' said
Jimmy sadly, blinking back fresh tears.

Andy spoke up softly:

'Nature's first green is gold,

Her hardest hue to hold.

Her early leaf's a flower;

But only so an hour.

Then leaf subsides to leaf.

So Eden sank to grief,

So dawn goes down to day.

Nothing gold can stay.'

The others looked at him in wonder, completely speechless.

He shrugged. 'Robert Frost. It's my mum's favourite poem. It felt right because of the circle of life and all that – that nothing lasts forever.'

'That was beautiful,' Anna said, giving Andy a pat on the back.

'Mum saw a fox eating dead fish at the back of my grandad's house,' Billy said. 'And I'm pretty sure I found the same fox lying dead by the side of the road the next day.'

'You're right, Billy. It won't just be the fish that are suffering if something's wrong with the water,' Jimmy said. 'Without safe water, nothing can survive.'

A little while later, they arrived at the neighbouring village of Whittle-on-the-Lye.

'The path by the river up there seems quite narrow,' Jimmy said, pointing further ahead. 'Maybe we should stash our bikes here and follow it on foot.'

They all hid their bikes in a nearby bush, then made their way along the path.

After a few minutes, Andy was the first to point out a makeshift raft built from wooden pallets and a couple of old oil drums, moored at a jetty behind the bowls club.

'Shall we?' he asked with a smile.

'I'm not sure we should steal from other people –' Billy began to say.

Anna interrupted him. 'But we could just borrow it? I mean, this is a pretty important mission, Billy. We have to complete it for everyone's sake . . . even the bowls-club members.'

'I'm not sure,' said Billy nervously.

'Oh, go on, Billy. We'll bring it back,' said Anna as her fingers formed into a beak and her hand became the formidable pecking bird. 'You know you want to, you *dooooooo*!'

As she started to peck Billy in the stomach and the neck, he couldn't help but giggle. 'OK, I do! I do! Anything to stop that awful bird, Anna!'

Andy grinned. 'There's lots of brambles ahead, so this is probably the safest way to travel.'

They climbed carefully on to the raft, making sure they were balanced and wouldn't tip into the water, then Jimmy unhooked it from the jetty and they set off upstream, eyes peeled for clues.

It wasn't easy to paddle the raft against the flow of the river, but eventually they fell into a rhythm. After about ten minutes, things started to become more eerie. They noticed more white lines burned into the riverbanks ahead of them.

'Billy, grab that branch,' Jimmy said, pointing to an overhanging tree. 'Let's stop and take a closer look.'

'There're more dead fish,' Anna said glumly, pointing to the shapes floating near the edge of the water.

'Poor things. And doesn't it seem really quiet?' said Billy. 'I'm not sure I like it.'

'You're right. There are no insects buzzing or any natural hum of the undergrowth,' Jimmy said

Billy flipped his hood up to use his binoculars. He noticed dark swirling water in the river ahead and followed it until a big, ugly pipe came into view.

'I've spotted something,' he told the others, 'and I think we need to get away from the water.'

They did as he said, tying up the raft before carefully clambering up the riverbank.

Billy pointed up the path on their side of the river. 'That's what I saw through my binoculars. Check out that pipe!'

They all looked in horror at the gushing green-tinted gunk pouring into the river, rubbing their eyes, which had started to sting.

'Let's keep back. It looks like a sluice gate to me,'
Jimmy said.

'A what?' Andy asked.

'It's something used by farms and other places to
control the flow of water – see how it's got a padlock
there? That's to stop anyone who doesn't have a key
from closing it.'

'But should it be pumping out stuff like that?'
Billy asked.

Jimmy shook his head. 'No, this doesn't
look good at all. I don't know what's

coming out, but can you see how the pipe's been freshly dug into the soil all the way up this field and beyond? That means it must be quite new.'

'Come on. Let's follow it and see where it goes,' Billy said.

'It smells so bad,' said Anna, holding her nose. 'Even worse than your bum, Andy,' she added, trying to relieve the tension, but no one was in the mood for jokes. This was all too scary and weird.

They followed the line of the pipe in silence. After about a quarter of a mile, they turned a corner and were faced with an ominous-looking building at the top of the hill. Dark smoke was billowing out from a large chimney, and the smell that had lingered in the air as they walked was stronger than ever.

They all looked at each other.

'What now?' asked Jimmy.

'We've come this far,' said Anna. 'I think we need to get inside and see what's happening.'

Billy took out his binoculars again. 'I can see two people on forklift trucks shifting stuff about, but if we head over to the right it looks like we can sneak past them. There's a big pile of pallets we could climb up to get over the fence, but I don't know how we'd get out again.'

'Let's worry about that later,' said Andy. 'If there are people around, we need to do this quickly, or we'll be spotted.'

They exchanged a look that said: *Let's do this!*

Billy and his friends pelted up the field, niftily climbed up the pallets and, one by one, jumped carefully over the barbed-wire fence. They found themselves in a courtyard full of sacks, pallets and barrels. Luckily, there didn't seem to be anyone around.

'What's that?' asked Andy, pointing to a barrel with a skull and crossbones on it.

'It says chlorine,' replied Jimmy, shaking his head. He started reading out a list of warnings: '"Toxic, harmful, explosive, corrosive, dangerous to the environment." None of this is good, and there's tons of it. Billy, have you got your camera?'

Billy whipped out his trusty Polaroid and took a photo of the barrels. 'I'll keep it handy in case we see anything else.'

As they sneaked onwards, they could see vats of all kinds of chemicals, each with the same skull-and-crossbones symbol, and most with long names they couldn't even guess at pronouncing.

'This is like a science lesson,' said Anna, her eyes wide.

The door of a giant shed in front of them began to open. Quickly, they darted behind a stack of barrels nearby.

A person wearing an all-in-one luminous yellow plastic suit with a gas mask over their face appeared. They looked like a scary astronaut.

'Why would someone need to be dressed like that?' Andy hissed.

They all watched as another person in the same outfit came out of the shed, wheeling a trolley covered in black plastic. A few feathers fluttered in the air as the trolley trundled forward. They couldn't see what was underneath the cover, and deep down they were all pretty glad about that. Whatever these plastic people were doing, it wasn't good.

Jimmy shook his head. 'I think we're on some kind

of massive farm. But chemicals like that shouldn't be just lying around or being pumped into the river. We need to get closer and find more evidence to help put a stop to whatever's happening here. It has to be what's upsetting the Rhythm. None of this is natural.'

'How are we going to get in?' Billy asked.

'Quick! Up here!' said Anna, racing up a flight of metal stairs that led to a huge spinning fan. The boys followed her, Andy more reluctantly than the others.

'I'm not sure this is a good idea,' he said fearfully. 'We can't go through there – we'll get chopped into tiny bits!'

'Not if we do this!' said Anna, opening a little box next to the fan. She twisted the lever inside and the fan immediately stopped. 'It's just the isolation switch. Standard.'

The three boys looked at her in amazement.

'My brother's an apprentice electrician. Luckily, he asks me to help him with his homework,' she said, smiling.

One by one, they quickly climbed through the gap between the blades. Billy tried to ignore his pounding heart and nagging thoughts that they were out of their depth. They had to find out what was going on here, so they could help the Sprites and the rest of Waterfall Woods – not to mention their own village!

They crawled along through a big metal tube, which seemed to be an air-conditioning pipe.

There was another awful smell in the air. Where were they? As they approached a big vent, Billy peered through and the others gathered round him. Below them was a giant laboratory of some kind.

'What's going on down there?' asked Anna.

Billy squinted between the metal slats of the vent.

'I can see people in white plastic suits with microscopes and syringes,' he said.

'It looks like a hatchery – I think they're breeding birds and incubating their eggs,' Jimmy said. 'Look, over there.'

They followed Jimmy's advice and saw thousands and thousands of gigantic turkeys caged on top of each other. The noise of the birds gobbling was so loud it could rival any football stadium on match day.

They watched as, every now and then, an egg rolled down one of many chutes to waiting trays.

They crept further along the pipe and could see through another vent into a room where thousands of eggs on trays were hatching.

Crawling along a bit more, they came across a bigger room, full of slightly bigger birds. It seemed to go on and on, the smell worsening as they moved further down the pipe. Next they came to a huge warehouse packed with turkeys.

They all stared through the vent.

'Does it look like the floor is moving underneath them?' Anna asked.

She was right. The floor was

like a giant, slow treadmill. A treadmill full of poop!
No wonder it stank in there. At the end of the room,
all the disgusting slop was being funnelled into a
pipe.

'Look – that must join up to the pipe that leads
to the river,' said Jimmy.

Just then, another door opened and someone
else in a plastic suit walked in. They shoved birds
out of the way, then pulled five wires down from the
wall and attached them to their suit. Reaching to a
green canister on their back, they grabbed a little jet
gun that was attached to it. With the touch of a
button, the figure was hoisted into the air. They
started to spray a fine mist over the turkeys while
gliding with precision back and forth over every
single bird.

Just like he had at all the other vents, Billy
pressed his camera up against it and took a photo of
the person in the air. Luckily, he had a trick where he
put the camera behind his hoodie binoculars, which
he used to magnify the photo, creating a precision
close-up. Genius!

'What was that?' asked Billy.

'I don't know,' said Jimmy, 'but it looked like some sort of chemical, which isn't good. Let's keep moving.'

Creeping along, they came to another series of vents. This time when they peered through they saw a small room full of TV monitors. Thankfully, no one was there, but the screens showed footage from the security cameras around the farm.

'We need to be careful,' said Billy. 'We don't want to get caught on camera. They seem to keep moving from left to right, so let's make sure we avoid them when we leave.'

They were about to move on when a man in a smart suit appeared on one of the screens showing the courtyard they'd just come through. He appeared to be yelling at all the people in yellow suits.

'He must be the boss,' said Jimmy as Billy snapped an image, capturing the man's face on camera.

'Got him,' said Billy. 'Let's get out of here!'

Scrambling on further through the pipe, they felt the air turn colder and the noise of the turkeys fell silent as they crawled past another room. This time, when they looked through the vents, the room was full of futuristic-looking machinery, with screeching noises coming from all the moving parts.

They could also see a spinning vat full of pink slime into which robotic arms were dumping vats of the chemicals they'd seen outside. The goo was then pumped through another machine that sent it down a tube. At the far end, it came out in large sheets from which thousands of little shapes were stamped out – nuggets, dinosaurs, rockets, footballs, moons, smiley faces and even twizzly little snakes. These were scooted along, breadcrumbed, and boxed up in bright packaging labelled: FARMER WHITE'S TURKEY BITES, with a picture of a pretty little barn, surrounded by flowers, a stream in the background, hills and a windmill.

'I recognize those boxes,' said Andy. 'We have those at home.'

'Us too,' said Anna.

'And at school,' said Billy.

'It's all a big lie, isn't it? I bet no one knows that

this disgusting factory is what's behind that cute country packaging,' said Jimmy.

'Or that they're pumping awful things into the river!' Billy added.

'Billy, you need to take pictures of this, too,' Anna said.

Billy nodded and held up his camera.

'We should leave now,' he said firmly after he'd taken a few photos. 'The longer we're here, the more chance we have of getting caught.'

They carefully crawled back the way they'd come, through the fan and out into the open air again.

Just as they got to the bottom of the metal stairs, they heard footsteps and quickly scrambled out of sight, slipping behind some crates, as two sets of big yellow boots and one set of flashy crocodile-skin loafers – no socks! – passed right in front of them. Hearts pounding, they held their breath.

Once the coast was clear, the four friends legged it back towards the fence. Billy had an escape plan – he pulled out the retractable harness from his backpack and slung the hook high over the fence, and round an overhanging tree, getting it lodged in a branch. Then they used the backpack to carefully swing over to safety, one by one. But there was no time to relax, and they kept running along the path all the way back to the river.

They only stopped when they reached the sluice gate once more. Panting, they tried to get their breath back and let what they'd seen sink in.

Finally, Jimmy spoke up. 'Everything bad that's being pumped out of that farm is travelling down this pipe and into the river, contaminating the water.'

'Well, we can put a stop to this at least,' said Anna. And she picked up a massive rock and tried to smash the padlock.

But it was no good. It wouldn't budge.

'Let me have a go,' Andy said.

Anna went to hand him the rock, but instead of taking it he simply twisted the numbers on the padlock dial. It popped open first time.

'How did you know the code?' Billy asked in amazement.

Andy shrugged. 'Whoever set the code didn't give

it much thought. I just tried one-two-three-four –
factory default setting – and got lucky. That's how my
dad had his motorbike stolen.'

Now that the padlock was off, Jimmy, Anna and
Billy heaved and pulled a big lever to shut off the pipe
spilling all the pollution into the river.

'This won't work forever,' said Jimmy. 'I reckon
we've only got a couple of days before it backs all the
way up the hill and floods the factory. Then they'll
know what's happened.'

'Come on – let's go home,' said Billy. 'We've done
all we can for now.'

They untied the raft, climbed back on and set off
back down the river. There was an ominous silence on
the journey back. The friends were in shock at what
they'd seen, just a stone's throw from their homes,
and no one knew about it except them.

Eventually Jimmy piped up softly, 'My neighbour's
been a farmer all his life, and he knows I'm interested
in nature so we talk about animals and farming a lot.
He told me once that we should be uncomfortable
when we think about eating animals, because we're

taking a life to feed ours. But we should also be able to trust that good farmers look after the animals in their care the best they can. It doesn't feel like that's happening at all at the farm we just saw.'

They fell into silence once more.

'It was awful,' said Billy. 'But at least we've definitely got to the root of the problem. And we have proof.' He held up a wodge of Polaroids.

'And we've stopped the sludge for now,' added Anna.

'So we just need a plan to shut down that "farm" for good,' said Jimmy.

'We should tell the Sprites, but I'm not sure our parents will be too happy if we're out late again. Let's take the raft back and go and see the Sprites tomorrow,' said Billy.

'But, Billy, we've all got the school trip to London Zoo tomorrow,' said Anna.

'I've been looking forward to that so much,' said Jimmy, 'but this is important. It can't wait.'

'Agreed,' said Billy. 'So how do we get out of the trip?'

'We need to fake letters saying we've got something contagious, something horrible that would spread really fast. I reckon norovirus will do it, and we all have to blame each other for catching it,' said Andy.

His friends looked at him, wondering what other letters he'd forged in the past. But it was a good plan.

'Now, we all need to have different pieces of paper, different coloured pens and different handwriting. This has to look and sound grown up,' instructed Andy as they sat in the treehouse an hour or so later, writing their notes. They'd raided the pub's stationery supply, so had plenty of options to choose from.

'Guys, my handwriting and spelling are terrible,' Billy said quietly. 'I'm never going to get away with this.'

'Don't worry, Billy,' said Anna. 'I can do yours. Just tell me what you want to write.'

Billy smiled at Anna – she always had his back.

'Once the letters are written, find something

your mum or dad has signed, hold it up to the window, then you can trace the signature. Easy as pie,' Andy said.

'How do we get our letters to the teachers?' asked Anna.

'We can slip them to some of the younger kids to take with them,' Andy replied. 'No problem at all.'

'That's the school trip sorted, but what do we do about the pollution?' asked Jimmy.

'I think we need some grown-up help,' Billy said, 'and I know just the man for the job. He practically lives in the pub – Jerry Draper, the local reporter. He's always wanted to break a big story, and this could just be it.'

'There you go, Billy!' said Anna. 'Who cares about handwriting when you come up with brilliant ideas. That's the Billy-Boy Way. So how do we do it?'

'Let's meet back here tomorrow morning at nine – make sure my mum and dad don't see you sneaking in,' Billy said, 'and we'll launch the next step of the masterplan.'

Chapter 7

Billy's Masterplan

'You OK, love?' Billy's mum asked the next morning as he sat down at the kitchen table. 'All ready for today's trip? London Zoo – that'll be exciting!'

'Oh yeah, Mum,' said Billy, pretending to be enthusiastic. 'Jimmy's hoping to make friends with some camels.'

'That's nice. You need a good brekkie before you go, and, as luck would have it, your dad's just back from the fruit-and-veg market. Look at all this!'

Right on cue, Billy's dad plonked a massive

watermelon, a pineapple, a mango and – the most unusual fruit of all – a starfruit on to the kitchen worktop.

'Mum's right – it's your lucky day, son!' he said with a smile.

Billy's mum picked up the biggest chopping knife you've ever seen and started peeling and slicing everything with ninja precision, creating a beautiful platter heaving with juicy fresh fruit. She had the most amazing ability to turn a pile of ingredients into a work of art. She made some sort of wonderful green dust in a pestle and mortar too, using mint leaves and sugar, and sprinkled it over the top. Meanwhile his dad grabbed a pot of yoghurt from the fridge and toasted some crumpets.

'This is so delicious!' said Billy as he tucked in. He then decided to broach the subject of Jerry Draper. 'Mum, do you think the guy from the local paper will be in the pub today?'

Mum laughed. 'Jerry Draper? Of course he will, love. At twelve p.m. on the dot, he always makes an appearance for his half-pint of beer, thimble of whisky, and scampi and chips in a basket. Same place, same time, every single day. But why are you asking about him?'

'Oh, there was a man yesterday who wanted to give him some information about a big national scoop,' Billy said.

'That sounds exciting,' Mum said. 'What did he look like?'

'He was wearing a fancy suit like James Bond! And he was carrying one of those new-fangled mobile phones,' said Billy. 'He was even driving an Aston Martin.'

'Wow! Well, I'll have to look out for Jerry Draper,' she said, winking at Billy's dad. 'Now, do you want me to turn these leftovers into a smoothie and pop it in a big flask for you to share on the school bus? It'll stay icy cold for hours – it's like the real deal Um Bongo,' she said, dancing around and humming the song from the TV advert.

Billy grinned. 'Yes please, Mum,' he said, knowing full well that they'd be enjoying that smoothie in Waterfall Woods, not on the school bus.

'Jerry Draper's never going to take us seriously –
we're kids,' said Anna when they'd gathered in the
treehouse to firm up their plan. 'We've got to do this
the right way.'

'I have an idea,' said Billy. He rummaged through
the piles of stuff lying around the treehouse. 'It's here
somewhere . . . Aha!' He pulled out an old typewriter
triumphantly. 'I knew this thing would come in useful
one day.'

'Brilliant!' said Jimmy. 'Stage one, we can use this
for the letter – then we don't have to write anything.'

Billy nodded. 'And let's put the letter in an
envelope along with the photos, like you see in
films. This is the big scoop Jerry Draper's been
dreaming of!'

They set about typing up everything they'd seen at
the farm. Jimmy wrote about animal welfare and the
devastation they'd witnessed and how it was affecting
the ecosystem, and Anna kept an eye on the language
they used to make sure it sounded proper grown up.

Billy found an old Ordnance Survey map, and he and
Andy used stickers to mark the farm's location. When
they were done, they stashed it all in a big manila
envelope.

Billy lit a candle.

'Why are you doing that?' asked Andy. 'It's broad
daylight!'

Billy smiled and poured wax on to the envelope
to seal it, stamping it with the Queen's head from
a penny. 'There you go – super professional. Right,

let's hide this in the pub and get to the phone box for stage two!'

At 12 p.m. exactly, the four friends were poised in the local phone box.

'Jimmy, this is your moment,' Anna said. 'Be posh, be smooth, be wise. Think James Bond.'

Jimmy cleared his throat as Billy popped the coin into the slot and dialled the pub's number.

'Hello, the Green Giant?' answered Billy's mum.

'Good afternoon,' Jimmy uttered in his deepest and best posh voice. 'I need to get an important message to a gentleman who goes by the name of Draper, Jerry Draper. A trusted reporter, I believe.'

'Oh yes! You're in luck – he's right here next to me. Who shall I say is calling?'

Jimmy panicked. The others looked at him blankly. They hadn't thought they would need to give a name!

'Um . . . it's Ron . . . Ron Bond,' he said.

'*What are you doing?*' hissed Anna. Surely Billy's mum wouldn't believe them now?

But, as she handed the phone over to Jerry, Jimmy
heard Billy's mum whisper in an excited tone, 'It's for
you, Jerry. Says his name is Ron Bond! I think he's
James's brother!'

'Hello, Jerry Draper speaking?' came the voice on
the line.

'Jerry Draper. I need you to listen. I have a BIG
news story for you. I'm a secret agent and have
uncovered something terrible.'

'What –' Jerry began, sounding very confused.

'There's no time!' Jimmy said calmly as Anna,
Billy and Andy tried not to laugh. Jimmy really did
sound like an important secret agent. 'What I've
discovered involves a corrupt farmer, pollution and
widespread damage. I've done my bit – months of
surveillance – to get to the truth. You'll find my
evidence in an envelope that I've hidden behind
the picture of Queen Victoria that I know you're
standing next to at this very moment. Read my letter,
look at the photos, then do your job, Jerry Draper.
This is the scoop you've been waiting for all your
life. This is your moment. Go to the big newspapers,

radio and television. I'm trusting you now to do *your* bit. Goodbye – never repeat my name, and you'll never hear from me again. Good day to you.'

Jimmy hung up, looking extremely proud of himself.

'Wow! Good job, mate,' said Billy, patting his friend on the back.

'He's definitely going to take that letter seriously,' agreed Andy.

'Come on. Let's get to the woods and tell the Sprites what's going on,' Anna said. 'We're not finished yet!'

'Something weird has happened . . . The compass has moved,' said Jimmy as they drew closer to the old oak tree. 'We were due north, and now we're due south. It doesn't make any sense.'

He retraced his steps,

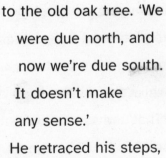

and Billy's compass swung back to north.

'Huh?' he said, walking back past the tree to his friends. Sure enough, the needle pointed south.

'Why would it do that?' asked Anna. 'It's like the other day when it was raining hard, then it suddenly stopped when we got here.'

'Never mind about the compass,' said Billy. 'Come on! We've got to go and talk to the Sprites.'

The friends raced on and, as they reached the Sprites' village, they found a flurry of activity. Everywhere you looked, Sprites were packing and moving stuff. There was a positive hum in the air and much excitement.

'Oh, Billy, yous is here!' said Basil, appearing as usual from out of nowhere and landing on his friend's shoulder. 'I told everyones all about what we found at Balthazar, and we held a vote and agreed to move there. It's where we should be, and it will be safer for us while the Rhythm is still offbeat.'

'That's what we need to talk to you about, Basil. We discovered what we think has been upsetting the

Rhythm, but we're trying to stop it. Please can you get Chief Mirren?'

Basil whizzed off and returned a moment later with the chief.

'Hello, our human friends,' she said. 'Basil informs me that you come with news about the Rhythm?'

'We found massive pollution in our river upstream of the woods,' Billy told her. 'It's coming from an awful farm, and we think that it might be the reason that your world is having problems.'

Chief Mirren and Basil looked shocked and upset.

'But we've stopped the pollution from going into the river, for now at least,' said Anna quickly, hoping to make them feel better.

'And we've done something to make sure that so-called farmer gets what he deserves,' Andy said proudly.

'The problem in our world,' said Billy, 'is that people don't always listen to kids. So we just need the grown-ups to do their bit. We think it'll work. The thing we haven't solved, though, is how the Boonas were able to come into our world. Because, in theory, that means more humans could come into yours, which we definitely don't want, right?'

Chief Mirren nodded. 'Thank you so much for all your help. I hope your actions will put a stop to the devastation that's happening,' she said. 'But you're right. We also need to understand why and how our worlds are colliding.

'Last week, Balthazar was folklore, and now we're working together to migrate to our real home. And Basil, Cassia and Rosemary told me of the Giant skeletons you found, too. All of which has made me wonder how many other tales I heard as a youngling might also be founded in truth.'

'What stories does you mean?' Basil asked curiously.

'There have always been stories of unique stones that can show some of the energy forces at work in our world,' Chief Mirren explained. 'I have heard that if you look through the holes within these stones, a gift you shall see. It is said that some might help foresee incoming weather, while others show people's true colours, their emotions – love, anger, their inner truth. It's even believed that one can show the beating heart of life itself – not just in animals but anything alive. I was never a believer in such fairy tales and fantasy. Until now . . .'

'So you want us to chase a fairy tale?' asked Jimmy.

'This fairy tale is all we have,' replied Chief Mirren. 'It describes stones – but no ordinary stones. These are meteorites from another world. Heavier, denser and magnetic. They landed in the waters of the highlands, then over thousands of years they have been pushed and tumbled down from the mountains, shaped, polished and hollowed by nature itself. They were used by many of old, but now no one possesses them. Beyond our realms is an area named Giants' Cove – this is where these magical stones are said to be found.

'There is one particular stone that could help us in our hour of need: the stone that can illuminate rips in time itself where you can see into different dimensions,' Chief Mirren said, raising an eyebrow. 'The legends suggest it is only lightning or the force of waterfalls that have the powers to cause such

tears. And this stone, I believe, is our only hope.
It could show us where our worlds are colliding,
where we need to go to fix it.'

'She sounds like Princess Leia in *Star Wars*,'
whispered Andy, and Anna gave him a look.

'Even I's never heard of these stones or the Giants'
Cove,' said Basil.

'The stones are rarely spoken of,' said Chief
Mirren. 'I've never believed them to truly exist. And
the Giants' Cove is in an area far beyond our reach
usually, because you must pass right through the
heart of the Boonas' territory and across hard terrain.
But, if we want to find the stones, I think that's where
we should look.'

'We'd love to help,' said Billy resolutely. 'Leave
it to us!'

'Thank you. But I warn you, it won't be easy to find
Giant's Cove.'

'We've got a map,' said Jimmy proudly, pulling one
out of his pocket. 'Perhaps that can help us?'

'That's not a map of our woods,' said Chief Mirren
gently. 'It's a map of *your* woods.'

She gave a nod, and a flurry of Sprites lifted the
map out of Jimmy's hands, turned it over and started
sketching with little bits of charcoal and pollen.
The friends watched in wonder as a vast
landscape grew on the paper in front of them,
from the clearing to the Boonas' territory and the
mountains surrounding Balthazar, to beyond. At the
edges were some areas of smudged black charcoal.

'What are those?' asked Jimmy.

'Some places even us Sprites hasn't ever been to,' said Basil. 'Those is best avoided.'

'There's no time to waste,' said Chief Mirren. 'You have the flint if you need our help, and I will also send my fastest Sprites to fly ahead of you, providing enough distraction to get you past the Boonas. Good luck.'

'Thank you,' said Billy gratefully. 'We won't let you down.'

The friends set off, with the other Sprites eagerly waving them on. A team of Sprites, including Basil, zipped ahead, with the four children following quickly behind.

They soon reached the Boonas' land, and the kids looked on as the Sprites jumped into action to distract them. They had perfected the art of getting the Boonas' attention, giving them some cheeky banter, dive-bombing low so that the Boonas would try to catch them, swooping through their hairy legs and arms and causing chaos, all the while moving the stinky things further away from the children so they were able to creep past quietly and unseen.

Once they were sure that Billy and the others were safely out of sight, the Sprites started their final flurry of action, so all the Boonas jumped up in a last-ditch attempt to catch them. But all that resulted in was a dizzy pile-up of bruised and battered Boonas as they banged heads!

With smelly danger now behind them, Jimmy focused on following the new map, but, as they got deeper into the woods, the friends got confused.

'Let's stop for a minute and think,' said Billy. He passed round the flask of tropical smoothie his mum had made – still slushy and super refreshing.

'What is this? It's amazing!' said Anna, Jimmy and Andy in unison.

'It's tropical fruit. Dad got it from the market. Mum just blitzed it with ice and a few secret ingredients. Bonkersly delicious, isn't it?' said Billy, grinning.

Everyone went in for seconds, and Billy started counting down: 'Five, four, three, two . . . brain freeze!'

Right on cue, they all raised a hand to their

forehead, going from pleasure to pain and back again.

'It's worth it,' Anna said with a laugh.

Back to business, Billy had a good idea. 'Over there –' he pointed – 'we'll get a better view of where we are.'

They climbed to the top of a hill, and Jimmy, Andy, Anna and Billy crowded round the map to work out their position. They seemed to be edging towards one of the smudgy black areas of the map.

While they were puzzling over it, they were interrupted by a low sound.

'Can you hear that?' Billy asked his friends.

They all stopped and listened hard. The air was vibrating with an enchanting, deep humming.

'Be careful,' warned Anna.

As the friends looked at the beautiful panorama ahead of them, there was a rumble and the ground beneath them seemed to shake. The soil gave way, causing a landslide that sent the four friends screaming and skidding feet first, arms and legs flailing, down the other side of the hill. They landed in a muddy heap, dazed and confused.

As they checked on each other, Andy wandered off into the trees. 'Guys, I can still hear something!' he called.

The others went to join him. Sure enough, the humming got louder and sounded less like humming and more like singing. And in fact they could now hear songbirds and whistles too.

'What is it?' asked Jimmy.

'Let's check it out quickly,' said Billy, starting to move through the trees in the direction of the sound. Anna, Jimmy and Andy followed eagerly behind.

It sounded even more beautiful the closer they got.

At last the trees cleared, and they found themselves faced with a huge, intimidating stone wall.

It stretched upward into the sky and seemed to go on forever in both directions. The strangest thing was that they hadn't seen it from the hilltop.

'What is this place?' Andy said. 'A prison?'

They all looked at each other. One thing was for sure: the singing was definitely coming from the other side of the wall.

Like a rat up a drainpipe, Anna scampered up a tree until she could peer over the wall.

'Wow!' she exclaimed. 'There's a beautiful garden! It's huge!'

'How big?' called Jimmy.

'At least as big as two football pitches!' replied Anna. 'Wait . . .'

'What is it?' asked Billy, frustrated that he couldn't see.

'I can see a Giant!' whispered Anna, suddenly lowering her voice. 'He's humongous. Nearly as tall as the wall!'

Chapter 8

A GIANT Mystery

They all clambered up the tree to join Anna so they could take a look at this almost unbelievable sight. Chief Mirren had told them that Giants no longer existed, but right in front of them was a real, live singing one . . .

So let's get a move on
And grow together.
Show the mud some love
In any kind of weather.

We'll grow, grow, grow,
Grow, grow, grow!

With just a little sun
And just a little rain,
With just a little love
And just a little pain . . .

We'll grow, grow, grow,
Grow, grow, grow!

There's magic here in the woods
And I'd find more if I could,
But I'm stuck inside these walls,
These godforsaken walls

But you guys are my everything.
You make me happy,
make me sing . . .

We'll grow, grow, grow,
Grow, grow, grow, grow, grow, grow!

The kids were spellbound! Partly because there was no doubt the Giant had an enchanting voice (and who knew Giants could sing?!) – but also because he seemed to be speaking to every living part of the garden. Swarms of bees that were lazily hanging in the air seemed to hum along to every note the Giant sang; neon-coloured birds the kids had never seen before were joining him in the chorus; strange-looking animals were pulling their long tails tight and playing them, making different sounds; and pink-spotted frog-like creatures were croaking rainbow bubbles into the air. Even more surprising was that the flowers had turned their heads towards the Giant, almost so they could hear him better, and their colours were vibrating to the beat!

The whole place was full of these breathtaking noises of popping, chirping, bopping and burping, as everything joined in. The sound was all around them. It was as if this gentle Giant was a conductor, orchestrating nature into a chorus of great growing. It was magical! The kids just stood with their mouths open – it was the most epic, inspiring thing they'd ever witnessed in their whole lives. 'We've got to get his attention,' said Billy, closing his mouth.

'What do you mean, *get his attention*?' replied Jimmy in a panic. 'He's a *GIANT*, Billy! What if he tries to eat us or something?!'

'I've just got a feeling he's . . . nice. Remember that Giants and Sprites lived together once? Maybe he can help us find the stones,' Billy said.

'Jimmy's right,' Anna said. 'Shouldn't we be a bit careful? I mean, the Boonas were awful, and this Giant could squish *them* with his little finger!'

'Well, at least there's a wall between us. I say we see if he can help,' Billy argued. And, without waiting for an answer, he called out in his most polite voice: 'EXCUSE ME! MR . . . GIANT! OVER HERE!'

'What's that? Who's that? Where are you?' the Giant hollered, looking around, panicked and a bit excited all at the same time. 'Where are you? Let me see you – give me a sign!'

Billy looked at his friends, silently urging them to help. Anna, Jimmy and Andy shrugged. It was too late now.

'HELLO!'

'MR GIANT!'

'OVER HERE!'

'IN THE TREE!'

They all shouted and waved their arms, hoping to catch his eye.

'Oh, I see you! Over there!' The Giant laughed, waving to them in amazement.

He hopped, skipped and jumped over to the wall – surprisingly nimble and light on his feet for someone so big – and peered up into the branches. Shocked to see humans, but happy nonetheless, he stuck out his big hand and said, 'I can't believe it. Look at you lot! I'm Bilfred. Nice to meet you.'

Bilfred must have been at least twice the size of the kids, with a big bushy beard and kind, soft eyes. His clothes looked like they were made from scraps of fabric, all carefully sewn together. Some might have thought he was scary, but he had such a gentle energy that you couldn't help but feel at ease.

Billy bravely reached out and shook hands with Bilfred. His eyes widened and his jaw dropped as his hand was swallowed up, and he realized just how small he was compared to the Giant on the other side of the wall. Now he understood how Basil must feel next to him.

'I'm Billy, and this is Anna, Jimmy and Andy,' Billy said, pointing to each of his friends in turn.

'It's so good to meet you. I can't quite believe you're real,' said Bilfred.

'We can't believe *you're* real! An actual Giant . . .' said Andy.

'I'm not a Giant. I've just got big – but I'm friendly, I promise,' said Bilfred, smiling. Then a look of sadness crossed his face. 'But I haven't spoken to anyone for a very, very, very long time. I sing to my garden family every morning, which starts the day off on the right foot, brings everyone together and helps to keep my head screwed on. Please come into my garden!'

'How long have you been here?' asked Anna.

'I'm not sure. It feels like almost forever. I was trapped in this garden when I was young and small like you! It's nearly all I've ever known.'

'That's so sad,' said Jimmy. 'You've been stuck here

for years all on your own?'

'Well, at first I cried and cried, because I couldn't find a way out. Day by day, though, I realized I wasn't alone and I learned to live with my little paradise. You might not be able to see it, but this garden is full of life!' Bilfred's face lit up again as he talked. 'And the living things come in all shapes and forms, speaking all different languages – some I do understand and some I don't, but that's OK. We always work it out in the end.'

'Shall we ask him about the stones?' whispered Jimmy, nudging Billy.

'What's that?' asked Bilfred. His big ears could pick up anything!

'Well,' said Billy, 'we're supposed to be looking for some powerful stones with special holes.'

'Powerful stones? Well, I've got a very big collection of stones. You're most welcome to come and have a look. They're everywhere in this garden – you've just got to know where to find them.'

Anna nodded eagerly. 'But how will we get in? This wall is way too high even for me to jump from.'

'Easy!' said Bilfred, extending his arms. 'I'll catch you!'

'I'll go first,' said Anna, bravely taking a leap of faith straight from the tree on to the wall and down into Bilfred's outstretched arms. 'That was fun!' she called up to the others. 'Come on – don't be scared!'

Billy went next, followed by Jimmy, and last but not least, with a little coaxing, Andy.

Once they were all over the wall, Bilfred turned, did a cartwheel and was off, the children running behind to keep up with his gigantic strides.

He led them to a wooden cabin in the middle of the garden. There was a wisp of smoke coming from the chimney, and the smell of freshly baked bread floated from the open door. Behind the cabin they could see the most amazing patch of land growing veggies of all shapes and colours.

Bilfred pulled a purple carrot out of the ground, which was as long as Billy!

'Wow!' said Billy. 'That would feed everyone in the pub for a week!'

'It's the amazing food and the life in the garden

that's caused me to grow like the clappers. Look – I even make my own shoes!' Bilfred said, and he pointed to the most eccentric-looking boots you've ever seen, feathers sticking out all over the place.

'I might be big now, but, like I said, I used to be the same size as all of you. The soil here is everything – once you start eating veg and fruit from this garden, you'll be the same size as me in no time. It's like rocket fuel!' And he pointed his hands in the air to make a rocket shape and dived into a compost heap, disappearing completely before exploding out of the other side.

The friends looked confused. They knew they should eat their fruit and veg, but they didn't know it could make them grow like that!

Jimmy piped up: 'It's not as weird as you think actually, guys. We know for a fact that some of the biggest dinosaurs on the planet were plant-eaters. The plants they ate millions of years ago must have been packed with good stuff. That's why the dinosaurs got so big. Maybe the soil in this world is just better than ours.'

'Well, that makes sense. We've seen the damage just *one* farm can do by polluting the water, and that's only the tip of the iceberg. Clearly, in this world, things are more full of life,' said Andy, running his fingers through the soil. 'And they definitely taste better,' he added, taking a bite out of the end of the massive purple carrot.

Billy and Anna looked at him, a bit surprised – Andy always came out with something ever so simple yet surprising when you least expected it.

'It's like paradise,' Jimmy said to Bilfred, blown away by the epic diversity of nature around him.

'It is very beautiful,' Bilfred agreed, 'but I do long for my own roots, my own life.'

'We'll be your friends,' said Anna with a smile. 'We'd love to come and visit you again.'

'Oh, would you?' asked Bilfred. 'Really? We can have so much fun.'

And, with that, he picked up Andy, and gently threw him into the air like a ball.

Andy yelped and let out a panicked fart, which propelled him just a little bit further.

Bilfred caught him easily as he fell. 'I'd better watch out for you, Andy!' he said, chuckling.

'Bilfred, I'm so sorry to rush you, but please can you show us the stones?' asked Billy.

'Of course, my new friends. Just give me a minute.' Looking around, he let out a high-pitched whistle, then held a finger up in the air.

The most extraordinary colourful bird landed on his outstretched finger. Bilfred took a big, juicy, wriggly worm out of his top pocket and handed it to the bird.

As the bird started to gobble it down, Bilfred tutted.

'Hold on a minute there. It's not all for you,' he said, pulling half back. 'Where's your wife?' he asked, as another bird landed on his head. He held up the remaining piece of worm, still wriggling, and dropped it straight into her beak.

As they flew off, Bilfred said, 'My dad always looked after my mum. He'd say, "Feed the ones you love; don't forget your manners."' He chuckled to himself as the friends looked on in awe. 'Anyway, come gather round.'

They all sat in a circle, as Bilfred opened a wooden

trunk. He had a good rummage around and pulled out four stones. A pearly white one, a shiny black one, a deep red one and a beautiful green one. Each of them had a hole in the middle.

'My garden has taught me that nature and life are all about harmony,' he said.

Billy nodded. 'Our friend Basil told us the same thing,' he said. 'The Sprites call it the Rhythm.'

Bilfred's eyes lit up 'Sprites are real?! You know a Sprite? I've only ever read about them in stories from the books in my library. I thought it was make-believe.'

'Oh no,' said Billy. 'Sprites are real, and they're ever so nice. If we can get you out of this garden, we'll take you to meet them.'

'I'd like that very much. And your Sprite friends are right. As part of this Rhythm, natural forces or energies seem to come in fours. The four phases of the moon. The four elements: earth, water, fire, air.'

'The four directions on a compass!' Jimmy interjected eagerly.

'Yes!' Bilfred said with a smile. He held out the black stone. 'When I look through this stone, I can see where all my little creepy-crawly friends are, day or night.'

'Wow! That's amazing!' said Jimmy. He took the stone from Bilfred and stared through the hole in the

middle. 'Hey! I can see super-sized ants, and the
biggest, never-ending multicoloured centipede. And
hang on – what on earth is that bouncing around?
It's like a cowpat with eyes!'

'Oh, that? It's just a beedleburp,' said Bilfred. 'Now
she is brilliant. Any mess, anywhere, and she'll see it
with those beady eyes, blast a burp, land on it, hoover
it up – and you know what happens next? At six
o'clock every evening – she *is* regular!' he said with a
wink, '– she gives me a pile of golden nuggets, and
when you scatter those among the veggies, they go
bonkers! Every home needs one, I'm tellin' yer.'

'Amazing! Mum would love that – and you don't
even need to plug her in!' said Jimmy.

'Let me have a look,' said Anna, and Jimmy passed
her the stone. 'Oh wow! This really is amazing,' she
echoed.

'Yes, and you wait till you look through it on a full
moon or during a thunderstorm,' said Bilfred. 'It gets
even more magical.'

Next Bilfred lifted up the white stone. 'This one
gives me a little head start on the weather. I can tell

it's going to rain before the drops start falling. It helps me to know when my garden needs watering, or when I can let nature take over. Today is such a beautiful day you won't see much. When the weather's on the turn, though, I always know about it well in advance.'

'What about the red one?' asked Billy.

'I think that one is for feelings. Not having had many visitors before you, I've only been able to look at myself, but I see different colours depending on my mood. Here, have a look.' He handed it to Billy. 'I'll be yellow, I reckon, as I'm so happy to see you.'

Billy looked through the hole and saw a big aura of yellow around Bilfred's head. But, as he looked down Bilfred's body, Billy could see that Bilfred's heart was blue with a blurring of green in the middle.

Bilfred might say he's happy, Billy thought, *but it looks like he's hiding a lot of sadness.*

'The green stone must be the one we're looking for then, I think,' said Jimmy.

'This old thing?' Bilfred replied, putting it up to his eye and peering through the hole. 'I have no idea what it does. It feels heavier than the others, though. I keep looking through it, but I don't ever see anything different. But, then again, I've never been out of these walls, so what do I know?'

'Please could we borrow it, Bilfred?' Billy asked. 'I think it might be the one we need.'

'Borrow it? You can *have* it, my friend! Take the whole lot. I've got loads of these things kicking about.'

'Thank you so much! We'd love to stay and talk some more, but this mission is urgent. We really need to get going – we've got a big problem to solve.'

'Can't you please stay a bit longer? Don't leave yet – you've only just arrived.'

The four friends looked at each other guiltily. They felt terrible leaving poor Bilfred alone, but they needed to get back to the Sprites with the stones.

'We're sorry, Bilfred,' said Billy, 'but we really have to go. We'll come back as soon as we can and we'll do our best to help you get out.'

'Yes, we promise,' Anna added. 'We're friends now, and friends don't break promises.'

Bilfred smiled. 'Friends,' he said. 'Well, as your

friend, my advice when faced with a problem – and it sounds like you have an important one to solve – is to retrace your steps, because sometimes the answer lies at the beginning of things.'

'Bilfred, have you ever tried to escape from this garden?' asked Andy.

'I've always wanted to be free, but the wall has always been taller than me,' replied Bilfred.

'And what do you do with all the food you grow?' Jimmy asked. 'Surely you can't eat it all!'

'When I got fully grown, this little red door in the wall started to open. It's far too small for me to get through, but every day after sunset I fill up huge long trunks with veg, fruit and herbs, chopping up any that are too big, and push them through the door. And every morning, when I wake up, the veg and fruit are always gone. I don't know who takes it, but they always leave nice things in return, like cheese and butter and fizzy apple juice and material I can make clothes with. In the beginning I was growing so fast that I had to keep adding extra bits to keep up,' Bilfred said, pointing to his patchwork jumper and trousers. 'Everything else I need, I've got here. So I just keep doing what I've always done, which is grow and cook and eat and sing.'

'Hmmm, another mystery! These woods are full of them,' said Anna.

'Have you ever tried to see who's taking the food?' asked Billy.

'If I stand too close to the door, they wait until I've gone to make the swap. Or, even worse, they punish me by holding back the nice treats, and – and . . . well . . . I like the nice treats!' Bilfred said, patting his tummy. 'And the special apple juice – that always makes me happy.'

'I know – why don't we try leaving through the red door?' suggested Billy. 'That way we can see if there are any clues.'

'Oh, thank you,' replied Bilfred gratefully. 'This way!'

He walked them back towards the wall, pausing halfway to say hi to a beautiful one-eyed chameleon, decorated with green and iridescent purple stripes, which was carefully looking everyone up and down while sitting like a little gargoyle on a branch.

'All right, Goffy?' Bilfred said. 'He might look miffed, but he's actually the happiest chameleon I've ever met.'

Then he stopped abruptly. Billy and friends watched in fascination as a busy convoy of the most fantastical creatures and bugs in all shapes and sizes, carrying all manner of woodland undergrowth, passed before them.

'They're on the move again, building a new home cos old Snufflesnorter's been trying to snatch all their eggs, the rascal,' Bilfred explained to the kids. 'I don't blame him – they taste ever so much like sherbet, not that I'd tell my tiny friends that.'

Once he was satisfied that the creatures were safely out of the way, Bilfred showed the four children to the small door. By lying down, arms stretched forward, they could just about shimmy through, helping each other with a bit of pulling and pushing.

'Goodbye, Bilfred,' they chorused. 'It was so nice meeting you. We'll be back!'

'You've made my day!' he replied. 'Well, in fact, you've made my week. No, my month. My year. Actually, you've made my whole life!' he finished, tears streaming down his face. 'Promise you'll come back, please?'

'We promise,' they all said as the door closed behind them.

'No sooner were they here than they were gone,' came the muffled voice of Bilfred, talking to the garden beyond the wall.

Billy could swear he could feel the garden hum and vibrate in response.

I bet Bilfred isn't there by accident, thought Billy. *It sounds like he's been imprisoned in that garden, and someone is benefitting from all his hard work.*

It sent a shiver down his spine to think that anyone could do such a thing to poor Bilfred.

'There's enough food coming out of that garden to feed a whole village,' said Billy to the others.

They looked around to see if there were any clues as to who was collecting the food from Bilfred. There wasn't anything in sight except a narrow trodden path leading away into the woods.

'Follow the path of least resistance?' suggested Anna, starting down the track.

'You know, I keep thinking about what Bilfred said about retracing steps and going back to the beginning,' Jimmy said as they walked. 'I think he might be right.'

'Right how?' asked Anna.

'Well, remember the odd things we noticed at the oak tree when we came to the woods? The compass changing direction? The weather suddenly clearing?' Jimmy explained.

'And the odd feeling I had when I hugged the tree on our first day here . . .' Billy added, latching on to Jimmy's idea.

'Exactly! I think that this has all got something to

do with the oak tree. Bilfred's right – our answer lies
at the beginning.'

Andy laughed. 'Oooh, deep!'

But his laughter quickly faded as the path they
were on opened out into a little clearing where a log
cabin stood. It looked like a regular garden shed, but
the air around them felt still and strange.

'This seems a bit weird,' Billy said, thoughts of the
tree forgotten. 'That small door in Bilfred's garden and
now this cabin.'

'Maybe we've time for a quick look inside?'
suggested Andy.

'It might help us rescue Bilfred,' Billy agreed.

They went in. The cabin was filled with rows and
rows of leather backpacks hanging from the walls, all
with goggles attached. At the far end, they could see
nets, ropes and various traps stacked on top of each
other.

'What is all this stuff? Who's it for?' asked Anna
in wonder.

Billy lifted one of the backpacks down and
inspected it. It was heavier than he'd expected.

The others did the same, and they took them outside
to inspect them in daylight.

Billy took off his own backpack, allowing him to
slip one of the new backpacks over his shoulders.
There was a smooth icy-blue stone on each strap, and
when he touched them the pack immediately
tightened to the perfect fit.

Suddenly a whirring sound came from within, and a
pair of extraordinary mechanical wings spread open,
before a helmet and goggles swung into place.

'Wow!' said Anna. 'Quick, let's get them on!'

The other three scrambled to the backpacks and
did exactly the same.

'But how do we fly?' Jimmy asked.

Gently, Billy leaned his head back and he began to rise in the air. And wherever he turned his head, he went.

'Lean back,' he instructed the others.

Before they knew it, all four of them were flying higher than the surrounding trees, their wings buzzing louder than a swarm of bees.

'If you lean in different directions, you can direct the wings wherever you want to go!' Anna cried as they got to grips with the flying buzzpacks.

She was right! Billy leaned forward and surged in that direction, picking up speed as he did so.

He leaned to the right and found himself skimming over branches, heading back into the woods. Anna and Jimmy followed, whooping in delight. They were flying! Andy, however, hadn't quite got the knack and kept bashing into the treetops and getting in a muddle.

Despite Andy's mishaps, they were covering a lot of ground. It was so much faster than walking and they were able to fly safely over the Boona's territory without a worry.

'You know what?' Billy shouted to the others. 'I think we should head back to the oak tree and look into Jimmy's theory. We've got these buzzpacks, so we'll be there in no time.'

'Good idea!' Jimmy yelled back. 'Then we might have even more to tell Chief Mirren!'

Anna and Andy nodded in agreement, and they all sped through the skies, back to the big old oak tree where their adventure had started.

Billy leaned backwards, trying to slow down and lower himself to the ground. It worked, and within seconds he was standing in the clearing. The others landed gently beside him. Well, apart from Andy –

he kind of fell to the ground. But, you know, practice makes perfect!

'Wow! That was amazing!' said Anna breathlessly. They pressed the stones on the straps, and the wings folded away.

'We'd better hide these,' said Billy. 'They'll definitely come in handy, but they're not ours. We need to return them at some point soon. We don't know anything about their owners. I don't think they're going to be our friends, and it doesn't feel right to take the buzzpacks out of the woods.'

Billy lifted Bilfred's green stone to his eye and looked through it. Everything was a little bit clearer, but with a twinkly tinge. And there, coming from the tree where the lightning bolt had struck, was a circle of glowing, shimmering light. Was this the window to the other world that Chief Mirren had talked about? The tear in time?

'I think we should call the Sprites,' Billy suggested. 'We don't know just how much this window has been affecting the woods, and Chief Mirren may want to be a part of what we discover.'

He reached under his top and held on tight to the flint necklace. He hadn't knowingly used it yet, but, when Basil had appeared to help him in the battle against Bruno, he'd just had to touch it and think about help, so he tried the same now, willing Basil and Chief Mirren to find them.

As they waited, Billy thought back to that very first day they'd come into the woods. Trying to remember what exactly they'd done . . .

'Hugging!' Billy cried.

'You want a hug? Now?' Anna asked.

'No! Listen, that very first day we went exploring, you wanted us to hug the oak tree as it was so old, Jimmy. Remember? Maybe that's what opened the window.'

'What window?' came a familiar voice, and Basil landed on Billy's shoulder, followed swiftly by Chief Mirren.

'It worked!' said Billy. 'I'm glad you got my message. We found the stone you told us about, Chief Mirren. We were given it by a Giant called Bilfred. Well, he said he wasn't a Giant, but he was huge and looked like one.'

'A Giant?' said Basil. 'No, no, no, yous must be mistaken. There's no Giants.'

'But there are, Basil! We just met him!' exclaimed Anna.

'Yes,' agreed Jimmy. 'He was lovely – very friendly.'

'A Giant!' said Chief Mirren. 'Goodness, we are learning a lot about these woods since you all arrived. There are many tales about the symbiotic relationship between Sprites and Giants –'

'What does that mean?' interrupted Andy.

'It means things work better together if they're interconnected,' said Jimmy. 'Like sharks and the pilot fish that clean them, who also get protection, or flowers and insects that need each other to survive.'

'All right, Nature Boy,' teased Andy. 'So it's like salt and vinegar crisps: you can't have one without the other.'

Chief Mirren raised a little eyebrow, cleared her throat and carried on. 'Tales of Giants have been passed down as legends, but no living Sprite has ever seen one, so there was no reason to believe in them. It seems, yet again, that we have been proved wrong.'

'Bilfred is very real, Chief Mirren,' said Billy. 'He gave us this stone, and it's showing energy around this big oak tree that was once struck by lightning. It might be the window between our world and yours. I've got an idea how to close it.'

'All right, Billy. Show us what you need to do,' Chief Mirren replied.

Billy handed the stone to Anna. 'You look through this, and I'll do exactly what I did before.' And, with that, he took a running jump and gave the tree a big bear hug.

Immediately after the hug, he turned round.

'Did you see anything?' he asked, but his friends and the Sprites were no longer there. It was just him, alone in the woods. Did this mean he was right?

There was only one way to find out . . . He jumped up and hugged the tree again, closing his eyes and hoping that this was the answer.

As he landed, he was incredibly relieved to find his friends waiting just where he'd left them, eyes wide open.

'Wow! What. Just. Happened?' said Anna.

'As soon as you hugged the tree, the glowing circle
I could see through the stone got bigger, then
disappeared – and so did you! Then the glowing
came back, and here you are again.'

That proved it! Somehow this tree had become
a way to open and close the window to this magical
world in Waterfall Woods.

'That's how the Boonas escaped!' Billy exclaimed.
'We left the window open this whole time. I'm so sorry,
Chief Mirren! This is all my fault – the Boonas, the
contamination. I think we've messed up the Rhythm.'

'Billy, wait,' Chief Mirren said in a reassuring tone.
'I do believe it's true that the window is the reason
the Boonas were able to enter your world and,
indeed, the occasional Sprite.' She turned to Basil
with a knowing look, and he smiled sheepishly.
'But, when it comes to the water, your actions
haven't harmed us. Quite the opposite, you might
have *saved* us.'

'Really?' asked Billy, his guilt easing.

Chief Mirren smiled at Billy and his friends.
'You have all helped us discover what's upsetting the
Rhythm and tried to stop it. And you've opened up a
whole new world of past, present and future, giving us
hopes and dreams. I've never seen our young Sprites
so energized. For too long, I think, we've been
concerned about keeping safe, but now we can see
there's a bigger world out there, and we have more
to offer.'

Billy listened to the chief's words, feeling his own confidence creep back. 'Chief Mirren, can I ask you a favour? We promised Bilfred we'd try to help him escape.'

She nodded. 'Bilfred has helped us all by gifting us this stone, so I believe it's our responsibility to assist him in return. Next time you return to the woods, we will devise a plan together.'

'Sorry to interrupt, but it's getting really late and, given that we're supposed to be on that school trip to London, we need to get back before our parents suspect we skived off today!' Anna said.

'You're right. We should go. But we'll be back soon,' Billy said. 'We promised Bilfred.'

They handed the magical stones to the Sprites for safekeeping, now that they knew exactly how to get in and out of the woods, carefully closing the window behind them, and swiftly made their way home.

Later that evening, Billy sat at the kitchen table, tucking into an absolute feast cooked up by his dad. He'd made perfectly pink salmon steaks, crispy little golden potatoes and a fresh tomato salad.

It was delicious, and Billy was starving after everything he'd been through that day.

'Tear some basil over those tomatoes, will you, Billy?' said Dad.

Billy smiled to himself and did as he was told.

'Now, how was the zoo today? Did you see everything you wanted?' Dad asked.

Billy panicked. He hadn't prepared an answer! So he went with the truth. 'There was a Giant in a big walled enclosure.'

'Giraffes? Oh, I love them – those lovely long elegant necks.'

'Little tiny buzzy Sprites. One even landed on my shoulder!'

'Beautiful dragonflies? I bet they were ever so delicate.'

'Not to mention the Boonas,' said Billy, getting into his stride.

'Boonas? Let me guess: porcupines or warthogs, darlin'? I love your imagination, Billy, but it would help if you actually learned the animals' names. That's the whole point of the school trip. You can't live in a fantasy world forever, you know, son.'

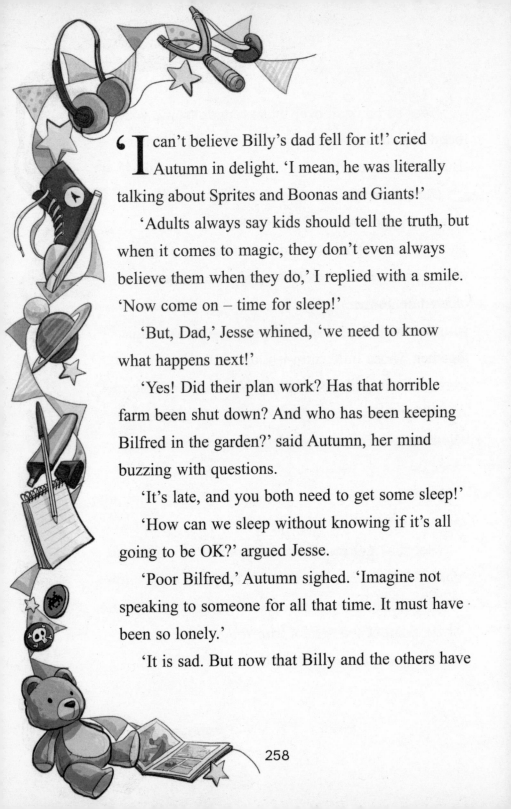

'I can't believe Billy's dad fell for it!' cried Autumn in delight. 'I mean, he was literally talking about Sprites and Boonas and Giants!'

'Adults always say kids should tell the truth, but when it comes to magic, they don't even always believe them when they do,' I replied with a smile. 'Now come on – time for sleep!'

'But, Dad,' Jesse whined, 'we need to know what happens next!'

'Yes! Did their plan work? Has that horrible farm been shut down? And who has been keeping Bilfred in the garden?' said Autumn, her mind buzzing with questions.

'It's late, and you both need to get some sleep!'

'How can we sleep without knowing if it's all going to be OK?' argued Jesse.

'Poor Bilfred,' Autumn sighed. 'Imagine not speaking to someone for all that time. It must have been so lonely.'

'It is sad. But now that Billy and the others have

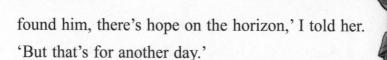

found him, there's hope on the horizon,' I told her.
'But that's for another day.'

The next night, we settled down as soon as dinner
was over and I was finally ready to tell the last part
of my tale. Somehow, being able to share this story
with the twins each evening was bringing us closer
together. Those little calm-ish, quiet-ish moments
were really important to all of us.

'We're ready, Dad,' Autumn said, nudging me to
begin, and so I continued . . .

Chapter 9

Operation Overnight

'**B**eefburger One here,**'** Billy said into his walkie-talkie early the next Saturday. **'Operation Overnight a success. I'm on my way to the woods – see you there! Over.'**

Operation Overnight – which meant telling their families they were staying at each other's houses – was something the four friends had put into action plenty of times before when they wanted to camp out without questions from the grown-ups. Today was the day they would try to rescue Bilfred, so being able to stay later without getting in trouble was a must.

Billy patted the bag at his feet, freshly packed with ropes, grappling hooks and winches he'd 'borrowed' from the garage last night – everything he could think of that might help Bilfred over that huge wall.

'Copy, Beefburger One. Operation Overnight a success here, too. Thunderbug is on his way. Over,' came the reply from Jimmy.

'Me too! Pretending to stay at each other's houses to avoid questions is the oldest trick in the book, but my parents didn't have a clue! Over,' said Anna.

'On my way too, Billy!' Andy's voice rang out.

Billy smiled and rolled his eyes. Andy could always be relied on to forget to say 'over' and use their radio names!

Keen to get going, Billy was determined to skip breakfast, but as he walked downstairs, backpack in hand, he was met with the smell of sweet strawberries bubbling away on the stove, and his stomach growled loudly. Boy, did Billy love strawberries! His mum always got locally picked ones from Norman's shop, then cooked them down until they were nice and

jammy. She served them up with big fat fluffy
pancakes and a dollop of yoghurt.

There was no way Billy could resist such a
delicious start to the day. Besides, a mission like this
demanded a satisfied tummy, right?

'Have you seen what's going on outside, Billy?' his
mum asked as she piled his plate full of pancakes
and jam.

Billy shook his head, his mouth already full of
yumminess.

'It's a right old circus,' his dad told him. 'Looks like
our Jerry Draper's landed a big story that's gone
national across all the weekend papers, and the whole
world has descended on the village!'

'I think he's finally got that scoop,' Mum chipped
in. 'It's the moment he's been waiting for.'

Billy raced to get his fill of the delicious pancakes
as quickly as possible before dashing outside to see
what was going on.

His parents were right. His usually sleepy village
was full of hustle and bustle. There were vans and
cars parked all along the main road, some with bright

signs that said things like **BRITAIN'S FAVOURITE NEWS** or **BRITAIN'S *ACTUAL* FAVOURITE NEWS**. There was even a helicopter circling overhead. The village square had been completely taken over – all because of the story they'd given to Jerry Draper. Surely this had to mean that the horrible farm would be shut for good?

Billy grabbed his bike and cycled across the square, dodging people as he went.

He passed the village shop and paused to read some of the newspaper headlines by the door. They ranged from the serious THE BIG CLEAN-UP STARTS: 100 MILES OF WATERWAYS AFFECTED to the more comical FARMER CROOKADILE SHOES and SEE YA LATER, ALLIGATOR.

Billy smiled – he knew that would make his mum chuckle. She was not a fan of crocodile shoes!

Just then, the mayor appeared, jostling with reporters, news crews and television cameras before scrambling up on to what looked like a hastily built platform.

'Ahem!' the mayor coughed, trying to get the

attention of the noisy crowd. 'This community will not tolerate pollution or any disrespect shown to our local wildlife and environment!'

Cameras flashed and whirred, and giant microphones were thrust forward to capture the mayor's words.

'I'd like to pass on our sincere thanks to local man and respected reporter, Jerry Draper, who was generous enough to share carefully gathered, robust evidence with the police at the same time as publishing his article in our local paper. The police have ensured that this dreadful crime and contamination have been stopped before they spread into neighbouring communities. There has been a recent influx of people admitted to hospital with breathing problems and stomach issues, who we now realize are all residents that live alongside the contaminated river. Rest assured, the "farmer" in question has been arrested and will be brought to justice. And all the animals on his farm have been removed by trusted local farmers.'

Jerry Draper stepped up on to the platform beside

the mayor, standing tall and looking very proud.
Photographers surrounded the pair, snapping away,
lights flashing.

I love it when a plan comes together, Billy thought
to himself. *Let's hope this means the Rhythm will find
its way again.*

Then, leaving the chaos behind, he jumped on his
bike and sped off to meet his friends.

Excitement levels were high as they walked up to the oak tree. Billy performed the special window-opening hug, and they were in. He closed it behind them – just to be safe – then they pulled out the flying buzzpacks they'd hidden, taking no time at all to pop them on and gear up.

Billy tipped his head back, a little more confident on his second go, and off they flew.

'The Sprites should have all moved to Balthazar by now, so let's head straight there!' Billy yelled.

The others nodded, and together they zipped through the sky, heading for the Sprites' new home.

Billy was so grateful they'd found these buzzpacks. As they glided high above the trees, he realized the immense size of Waterfall Woods, and just what a long journey it was to reach Balthazar on foot. He thought about all they'd uncovered so far, and wondered whether any other kids or grown-ups had ever had such an experience before.

As they flew over the mountain range near

Balthazar, the group slowed down, preparing to land in the courtyard in front of the castle. It took Andy a few goes of whizzing back and forth until he managed to set himself down next to the others.

The Sprites were always happy to see Billy and his friends, but they were really impressed when they saw their amazing flying buzzpacks.

'*Wowwwww!*' they chorused. 'Where did yous gets these from? Yous is flyin' around likes us now.'

'We found them in a cabin near where we came across our friendly Giant,' said Anna.

'Chief Mirren,' said Billy, 'our idea on how to fix the pollution is going to plan. Even in our world, people care about the Rhythm; they just don't always quite know how to go about it, as they're so busy doing other things.'

Chief Mirren replied, 'Just saying thank you isn't nearly enough gratitude for what you've done for the Rhythm. We could tell straight away that you'd done something meaningful. It was as if we saw Mother Nature herself take a big deep breath, giving life back to the woods – flowers starting to bloom again, the hum and buzz of the undergrowth returning. Things just feel happier.'

Billy, Anna, Jimmy and Andy beamed. When they first arrived, they hadn't thought that they could do anything to help the Rhythm because they were just kids, but now they were proud to have played their part.

'So we promised to rescue Bilfred. Do you think your magic can help him?' Billy asked.

'Sprite magic can do many things, but it's delicate, finite, and, if the wall is as high as you say, saving Bilfred from his garden prison may be harder than you imagine,' replied Chief Mirren. 'But we must try, so now that you have these buzzpacks, we can all fly together to avoid the Boonas on the ground, with you leading the way. Basil, will you please organize some refreshments for our human guests while we prepare to leave?'

'As you wishes,' said Basil with a smile. 'Refreshments comin' right up!'

'I wouldn't say no to a nibble,' Andy called as Basil flew away.

'It's only just after breakfast,' Jimmy said with
a chuckle.

Since the friends' last visit, the Sprites had
obviously been hard at work, cleaning and moving
things. The children sat down on the ground and
watched in wonder as, with a nod from Basil,
the Sprites started to bring over little snacks one by
one – nuts, seeds, berries and grapes – building up
beautiful bowls of goodies for them to enjoy. Basil
waved his arms and directed the other Sprites as if
he was conducting a gastronomic
orchestra.

One bowl, however,
stayed empty. Every time
the Sprites went to fill it
with juicy mulberries,
Andy and Anna would call
out, 'Over here! To us!' and the Sprites
dropped them, one by one, straight into their gaping
mouths!

'And something to drink!' said Basil.

To go with the goodies, a huge jug filled with

delicious drink, as well as lumps of mountain ice and slices of extraordinary-looking fruit, was flown over to them by what looked like twenty Sprites all working together.

They tried to pour Billy a glass, but it was frosty and slippy. Just before it spilled everywhere, several more Sprites rushed in to help steady the jug. It was a symphony of silver service.

'This is lovely,' said Anna between mouthfuls.

'Yumph!' agreed Andy, stuffing his face with fruit and nuts.

But Billy wasn't listening. He was too busy thinking.

'I've got it!' he cried. 'This is it – this is the answer.'

'What, good snacks?' asked Jimmy, looking at the spread before them.

'No,' said Billy impatiently. 'I mean, yes, they are good, but what else? How did it all get here?'

'Teamwork!' Anna cried, catching Billy's drift.

'Exactly! Like Grandad always says, "Many hands make light of heavy work." If twenty Sprites can lift a jug like that, just imagine what thousands of them could do!'

Basil grinned from little ear to little ear and winked at his friend. 'Now that sounds like a plan to me!'

A short while later, the entire Sprite population rose into the air alongside Billy, Anna, Jimmy and Andy in their flying buzzpacks. Chief Mirren was at Billy's side as he led the swarm of Sprites across the forest, the epic buzzing of thousands of wings filling the air.

Billy could feel that some of the Sprites were nervous as they sped down the valley, but he could hear Basil doing his best to reassure everyone, zipping about and making encouraging noises, especially to the younger Sprites who'd never flown this far before.

'There it is!' cried Anna after a short while, pointing out the approaching massive walled garden.

Billy scanned the landscape. There was no sign of Bilfred . . . Where was he?

It took a couple of seconds, then Andy said, 'There he is!' – pointing in the direction of a huge mound.

And there Bilfred was – lying like a starfish in the
sun, soaking up some rays and having a nap on top
of the steaming compost heap. Billy laughed and led
the way.

As the Sprites hovered overhead, blocking the
sunlight, Bilfred opened an eye, and Billy saw him start
to panic. Not knowing where to go, Bilfred turned over
and began burrowing into the pile of rotting veggies,

hiding his head, but leaving his bum in the air.

'Bilfred!' shouted Billy. 'Bilfred, don't be afraid!
It's your friends. And we've brought help!'

The Sprites, sensing Bilfred's panic, flew out
of sight.

Bilfred's face slowly emerged from the compost.

'Billy, is that really you?' he asked, pulling a
cabbage leaf from his ear. His eyes filled with tears,
a lone drop spilling down his cheek. 'You came back
for me.'

'Of course! We never break a promise. We'd never
leave a friend in need.'

'We're here,' said Anna, 'and we've got a plan,
right, Billy?'

'Why are you here with so many bees?' Bilfred
asked. 'That's what scared me. I've been stung really
badly before, and not in a nice place.'

Chief Mirren and Basil flew down to join Billy,
hovering just in Bilfred's eyeline.

'Bees?' said Basil. 'First the hoomans thought we's
fairies, and now you thinks we's bees! We's Sprites,
you know!'

274

'I do apologize,' Bilfred said, looking sheepish. 'I've never seen a Sprite before, let alone a whole swarm of them!'

'They're here to help get you out,' Billy explained. 'Bilfred,' he said earnestly, 'I'd like to introduce you to Chief Mirren, Basil and all the Sprite community.'

Basil landed on Billy's shoulder as the rest of the Sprites buzzed into view, cheering and waving their little arms.

'Hello, Bilfred, nice to meets you!' said Basil proudly.

'Oh yes, nice to meet you too, little Sprite,' replied Bilfred, 'but you don't have to whisper. Now, this is lovely. Like I said, I've never met a Sprite before, but I have read about when the Sprites and the Giants were best friends, because opposites attract, don't you know?'

'We have also heard tales of the friendship between Sprites and Giants,' Chief Mirren said kindly. 'And now we have discovered a whole magical place that proves they are more than just stories. Giants and Sprites once lived in harmony.'

'And it seems that humans can be pretty friendly, too,' said Bilfred, winking at Billy and the others.

'The humans are the reason we're here. Billy tells us that you've been trapped in this garden for many years,' Chief Mirren said, and Bilfred nodded sadly. 'Well, you gave us the stone we need to help understand problems we've been facing. So we want to help you in return.'

'I'm so pleased to meet you all, but – no offence to anyone – what are you little Sprites going to do? It's not like you can pick me up and fly me out of here, is it?' Bilfred chuckled, clutching his belly as he laughed.

'Well, actually . . .' said Billy, beaming, 'many hands make light of heavy work.'

He heard his words echo round the sky as the Sprites repeated the plan.

Bilfred took a deep breath to stop himself laughing, and, as he did so, all the Sprites surrounded him. They grabbed Bilfred's clothes, hair, ears, anything they could take hold of, and then, as they heaved and pulled with all their might, they lifted

Bilfred right off his feet.

Slowly but surely, Bilfred rose into the sky and away from the walled garden. Finally, he was being flown free of his prison, which was now gradually disappearing beneath him.

'I'm freeeee! Come and visit me, my friends,' he bellowed to the garden below, as little foxes, badgers and even the beedleburp lifted their heads in wonder to watch him leave.

As the Sprites strained and puffed to keep his big body afloat, Bilfred lifted his head and gasped. A glorious horizon stretched out in front of him. In the distance, the sun was setting, dipping down between the mountains, and the golden light reflected beautifully in all directions, bouncing off rivers and waterfalls. Bilfred had seen nothing but the wall blocking his view, and blocking his life, since as far back as he could remember.

'Wow! Look! *Look!*' he cried in wonder.

Billy watched with a grin – it was like Bilfred was a child again, giggling and looking in awe at the world beneath them. He turned to Anna, Jimmy and Andy

and saw that they all had huge smiles on their faces, too. With the help of the Sprites, they had done it. Bilfred was free.

As soon as they landed, Bilfred scooped up the four friends in his arms and gave them a big squeeze, saying, 'I can't believe it! This is the best day ever.'

'Tonight, Mr Bilfred, I thinks we should cooks you a feast,' said Basil.

'So this is the Balthazar I've read so much about
in my books. And Sprites are real, not just a fairy tale.
You're mythical creatures right here in front of me,'
said Bilfred.

'Well, no, actually, we's magical, not mythical,
Mr Bilfred,' said Basil.

Bilfred nodded. 'How can I thank you all?' he
asked, looking around. 'I never thought I'd set foot
outside the wall of my garden.'

'Bilfred?' Billy said gently. 'Would you tell us more about how you ended up in the garden?'

'OK, Billy. I try not to think about it too much, but I reckon I owe it to you to tell you what's out there in those woods . . .'

Chapter 10

Bilfred's Tale

A fter a flurry of action from the Sprites, the friends found themselves seated round a big table at Balthazar, with Bilfred on one side and Chief Mirren on the other (although their chairs were quite different sizes of course!). Working together in their wonderful way, hundreds of Sprites managed to safely manoeuvre a cauldron of bubbling hot broth to the centre of the table. Billy's nose twitched as the aroma of fresh spring veg filled the air, and he couldn't help but let out a long, low *mmmmmmmmmm*.

'Now what have you got in there?' asked Bilfred, equally eager to get stuck in. 'I see fresh perri peas, fudge beans . . . Ooh, and what's that? A whole lot of lovely green boondingles and swimmer beans – my favourite. Now, if I was making a soup like this, I'd say you need to add a sprinkling of –'

But Bilfred was stopped in his tracks as several Sprites zipped above the cauldron and scattered an array of fresh green herb leaves and flowers over the soup, finishing with a drizzle of oil.

Bilfred laughed. 'You're one step ahead of me!'

'Have you got any white sliced?' asked Andy, keen to move on from the theatrics and into the eating zone.

'White sliced?' asked Basil, looking perplexed.

'Bread,' explained Andy.

'Well, I doesn't know what "white sliced" is, but we does have breads.'

A group of Sprites buzzed over in tandem with the most unusual-looking bunballs in all sorts of shapes and sizes.

Basil grinned at Andy. 'We uses every kind of grains and oats to make these lovely breads all ready for dunkin'.'

'This looks amazing!' cried Billy, all his senses alive to the wonder of this occasion, candles burning, fireflies dancing in the moonlight.

'Before yous tucks in,' interjected Basil, 'tries some of our special seasonin'.'

Billy noticed that there were pinch pots dotted round the table, all different colours and each containing a different sprinkle. They were filled with delicious-smelling combinations of crushed nuts and seeds, herbs and spices.

'Now, once you've had your fill, perhaps you can share your tale, Bilfred?' said Chief Mirren encouragingly.

'Oh, I can eat and talk,' he replied, slurping his broth. 'Where shall I begin?

'Meeting the four of you reminded me I was human-sized once, too . . .' He paused and looked at Billy and his friends. 'Oh, I used to have such a lot of fun climbing trees, digging holes, making little camps to hide out in for the day. All with my one best friend. We loved these woods and all the adventures we had together.'

'That's just like us!' Jimmy said, smiling at the others. 'We do all those things too, and always with each other.'

'So how did you end up trapped in the garden?' Billy asked, suddenly worried. If Bilfred had once been just like them, what happened if they got stuck, too?

A lone tear escaped from Bilfred's eye and trickled slowly down his cheek, splashing on to the table and creating what to Basil and the other Sprites was almost as big as a puddle.

'I think I hid the memory for a long time because it was so hard. But ever since you four arrived in my garden I've been trying to think more and more about what happened to me when I was a nipper, and now I remember the day so clearly.' Bilfred gave a deep sigh.

'It's OK – we're here,' said Anna, putting her hand on his arm for reassurance.

'Me and my best friend were playing under the big oak tree at the entrance to the woods, as we always did, and we heard a rustling. It wasn't all that unusual because we quite often saw little rabbits and field mice scuttling through the undergrowth. But this was different – this was something new.'

Bilfred's tone changed, and they could sense the fear in his voice. Everyone – Sprites and humans – listened intently.

'The whole feeling of the woods seemed to change in an instant. It was like a darkness descended. We could hear this intense, haunting howling from all around us. My friend . . .' Bilfred screwed up his face in concentration.

'No, not friend,' Bilfred continued, looking round the table with sad eyes. 'My big brother! My brother knew something was up, and he took my hand and found us a hiding place in the undergrowth, holding me close. The rustling got louder, but we weren't fast enough. The most frightening creatures appeared and surrounded us – two-headed beasts! My brother told me to run and, even though I didn't want to leave him, I was so scared that I did as he said.'

Another tear fell from Bilfred's eye, and Billy reached out and put his hand on top of Bilfred's huge thumb.

'If it's too hard, then you don't have to tell us,' Billy said. 'But, if you can, then I hope that we'll be able to help you find out what happened to your brother.'

Bilfred nodded and wiped his eyes. 'I want to finish.

Bilfred's Tale

I've tried not to think about him for so long, but now
I want to share my – *our* – story with you all. I started
to run, and I heard my brother cry out. I turned and
saw that he was trapped against an oak tree,
surrounded by the beasts. I wanted to help, but I was
frozen with fear. Then out of nowhere a frightening,
fancy-looking lady in a long dress floated over to my
brother, and she just sucked his eye right out.' Bilfred
shuddered at the memory, making a *pop* sound with
his mouth, then he sank his head in his hands.

'Shocking it was. I can still hear it now – I'll never forget that sound.'

Billy and his friends stared at Bilfred in horror. What a horrible thing to happen, and in these woods!

But, as Bilfred spoke, in Billy's mind a thought started to form – could it be . . .

'Oh, Bilfred!' said Anna. 'That's awful! What did you do?'

'Well, my brother started to run towards me. He shouted for me to run again too, but, as I turned, something must have hit me over the head. The next thing I knew I was waking up in the walled garden, dizzy and confused and all alone. There was a pile of books, tools and fruit and veg next to me. For a while, I thought about nothing but my brother – I left him behind when I should have stayed! But, over time, I hid the memory. It was just too painful. That's why I focused on the garden and the wonderful animals and plants that surrounded me. I didn't deserve to escape when I'd run away from him. I should have stayed and protected my big brother like he always tried to protect me.'

Bilfred buried his head in his big, rough hands and started to sob.

'Tell us more about the garden, Bilfred,' Jimmy suggested gently, trying to distract him.

Bilfred raised his head and gave a sad smile. 'That garden became my best friend. I'm ever so pleased to be free of those walls, but, to be honest, the life inside them has been my family since that terrible day.

I've learned all about nature, and it's nurtured me so well for all these years, and I've got thousands of tiny little pals in all their weird and wonderful shapes and sizes.'

'Nature is really very special,' said Jimmy in firm agreement.

'That's why we alls has to protect the Rhythm,' chipped in Basil. 'We's got to do our bit, and in return the Rhythm will take care of us.'

'Are you OK, Bilfred?' asked Jimmy.

'Yes,' Bilfred said, nodding. 'I'm grand.'

'You can lie with your words, Bilfred, but not with your eyes,' Jimmy said gently. 'And your eyes look really sad.'

Bilfred looked up, confused. 'Wait a minute – I've heard that before. My mum used to say that all the time.'

Billy jumped up from his chair. Anna was also listening intently.

'Bilfred, can you remember exactly how many years it's been?' asked Billy, getting excited. He thought he might be on to something, and this might actually prove it . . .

'I don't know.' Bilfred scratched his head. 'Maybe fifty years or so. I used to keep track, but I gave up counting long ago.'

Billy looked at Anna, and she nodded in agreement. 'Is your brother's name . . . Wilfred?' Billy asked.

Bilfred froze, tears coming back into his wide eyes. 'How did you know that?'

'Oh, Bilfred,' said Anna comfortingly. 'Wilfred made it out of the woods that day. He escaped!'

'Anna's right!' cried Billy. 'We know him, and we know where he is. It all makes sense. He's alive and lives literally just outside the woods!'

'I-I-I'm lost for words,' Bilfred said, trembling as he tried to come to terms with the idea that his long-lost brother was so close yet so far away.

'Billy, please can you tell us more?' prompted Chief Mirren. 'Let us be certain that we are on the right path.'

'Of course,' said Billy. 'The Wilfred we know is
a very lonely old man.'

'Which makes total sense now,' said Anna
excitedly.

'Yes,' said Billy, nodding. 'I heard my mum say
once that he'd lost something, which is why he always
looks so sad. Now we know that what he lost was
actually *you*, Bilfred. And my grandad told me the
story of two brothers who went into the woods, and
only one came out – that's you two! I'm sure of it.'

'You're right, Billy!' said Jimmy. 'And it would
explain why Wilfred's always telling people not to go
into the woods. He doesn't want them to get hurt like
him . . . or lost like his brother.'

'Oh, and the small detail that he only has one eye!'
Andy said. 'The left one!' he added, pointing to his
face. 'It has to be him.'

'Yes, that'll be him,' Bilfred said, smiling through
the tears. 'I remember now . . . We lived in a house at
the edge of the woods! He must have never left home,
not wanting to move from the village . . .'

'It sounds to me, dear Bilfred, that this *is* your

292

brother, and it's clear he's never forgotten about you,' said Chief Mirren.

'Wilfred has been close to me all this time?' said Bilfred quietly, almost to himself. 'But just out of my reach?'

Billy nodded.

'Oh my,' said Bilfred with a smile, standing up from the table. 'Oh, what a day! First you rescue me, and now you tell me that my bestest big brother is alive and still living in the village. Oh, this is just marvellous.'

All the Sprites started zipping through the air, waving their arms about with glee.

'I need to see him now! How do I get to him?'
asked Bilfred, looking around wildly.

'I don't mean to be a party pooper,' said Anna,
glancing up at Bilfred, 'but you're a bit bigger than
everyone else back home. I don't think you can just
go walking around without being noticed.'

'Anna's right. Besides, the village is swarming with
journalists and news crews at the moment, so it's
definitely not the right time for a Giant to be making
an appearance!' said Billy. 'You'll be pounced on –
you'll end up with the police or the army after you.
And everyone would find out the truth about Waterfall
Woods, and it could mean the end of your world as
you know it. No, we need to bring Wilfred to you.'

'We can go and talk to him,' suggested Anna. 'But
I'm not sure he's going to believe us. Can you tell us
something that only you would know?'

'Hmmm . . .' said Bilfred, a thoughtful look on his
face. 'Well, I did have a secret hiding place up the
chimney, out of sight. I stashed an old biscuit tin up
there, and inside is Wilfred's precious clockwork
steam train that I fixed. I was going to give it to him

on his tenth birthday. I even made him a card. It should still be there.'

'Let's hope so,' said Billy. 'Finding that should do the trick.'

'We'll go there right now!' said Jimmy.

'Wait a moment,' said Chief Mirren. 'I know you're keen to help, children, but it's been a long and eventful day. And won't the grown-ups in your world be worried about you?'

'Forgive me, dear chief,' Bilfred said, 'but I'm not sure I can wait another day, and it sounds like my brother needs to know the truth, too.'

'It's OK, Chief Mirren,' said Billy. 'We're happy to help. And we don't want Bilfred and Wilfred to be separated any longer. We can use our flying buzzpacks to get back quickly and tell Wilfred what we know.'

'And we put Operation Overnight into action to make sure that we could stay and help for as long as we're needed,' said Anna. 'So our parents will be fine.'

'Then I wish you good luck,' said Chief Mirren,

looking impressed. 'For now, we will find somewhere
for Bilfred to rest.'

'Oh, thank you, Chief Sprite, but I'm not sure I'll be
able to nod off with all this going on. Are you sure I
can't go with you children?' Bilfred replied.

'Why don't you meet us by the old oak tree?'
suggested Billy. 'At the window between our worlds.
That way you'll be reunited as soon as we bring
Wilfred back into the woods.'

'Very well, you go and speak with Wilfred, and we'll
escort Bilfred to the tree and wait for your return,'
Chief Mirren replied.

Chapter 11
A Midnight Adventure

The four friends flew silently by moonlight above the woods, wasting no time to get back to the oak tree where they hid their buzzpacks as before.

They quickly jumped back over the wall and grabbed their bikes from the ditch, rushing to get to Wilfred's cottage as fast as they could. Now that they were near the old man's home, though, they felt nervous about what he'd say. Would he believe that his long-lost brother was as big as a Giant and had been living in the woods all this time? Especially when the news came from a bunch of kids.

They halted in front of the path to the cottage, looking at each other.

'I'm not sure if I can do this,' said Billy in a moment of self-doubt.

'We could always come back tomorrow – that old man frightens the life out of me, and I'm ever so hungry,' said Andy, sensing a chance to escape.

Anna squeezed Billy's hand. 'Come on, Billy. We've come this far. What's the Billy-Boy Way?'

Billy had started all this by deciding to explore the woods in the first place, so now he knew he had to see it through and complete the circle. Bilfred was relying on them. He dug deep, summoning up as much courage as he could muster. He breathed deeply and decided to take the lead.

'The Billy-Boy Way is to face this head-on and tell the truth. After all, he'll be able to see it in our eyes, remember. Come on,' he said. 'We just have to make Wilfred believe us!'

Anna, Jimmy and Andy smiled. 'After you, Billy!' Anna said, giving him a high five.

They all ran up the path, their excitement to reveal

the discovery overcoming any nervousness about old Mr Revel. Billy knocked on the front door.

No answer. He tried again, louder this time.

Still there was silence.

'Do you think something's wrong?' asked Jimmy. 'The radio and lights are on, so he can't be sleeping.'

'Let's take a look around,' suggested Billy.

They crept round the house, peering through each window they passed for clues. At the back, they found an open door leading to the kitchen. Billy sniffed, catching the smell of browning pastry and what he could swear was the combo of chicken, mushrooms and mustard. So where was Wilfred?

'Mr Revel!' called Billy. 'Hello, Mr Revel? Are you there?'

He stepped tentatively into the kitchen, the others following close behind. It was like stepping back in time to the 1930s. There was a wood-burning stove, copper pots and pans, old furniture, trinkets and tools that must have been there Wilfred's whole life. Billy had thought his grandad had loads of cool old stuff, but Wilfred's house was off the scale!

'Look at this old thing!' exclaimed Andy, picking up
an old piggy bank off a shelf and jangling it around.
'Loads of pocket money in there.' He went to put it
back and accidentally dropped it on the floor.
It smashed spectacularly into hundreds of pieces,
coins rolling everywhere.

'Andy, what have you done?' hollered Jimmy.

'It wasn't my fault,' insisted Andy. 'It just slipped
out of my hand.'

They all bent down to start clearing up the mess.

'Be careful,' Anna said. 'The pieces are super sharp.'

Jimmy was picking up coins near the doorway into the hall when something caught his eye.

He stood up. 'Guys, I think you're going to want to see this . . .'

The others followed him into a little room off the hall, which was plastered floor to ceiling with maps, newspaper cuttings and drawings of what looked like some seriously scary two-headed beasts. There were so many of them: some drawn in pencil, some painted, some sketched in charcoal. Every map was covered with pins, joined together with cotton, scribblings and checklists, as if someone was trying to dissect the woods and re-walk every square metre. This was clearly a lifetime's work. A shotgun was propped against the wall.

'Look at this,' said Anna.

She pointed to a newspaper clipping that showed a picture of a little boy, one eye bandaged up, looking sadly at the camera. The headline read: **BEWARE: CHILD ATTACKED IN WOODS BY DANGEROUS DOG.**

There was another clipping next to it with a photo of a smiling boy who looked like a smaller version of the other child. This one had the headline: CHOIRBOY BROTHERS MYSTERIOUSLY TORN APART: YOUNGEST GOES MISSING.

Billy looked round the room. It was as if the whole story of Wilfred and Bilfred was unfolding before his eyes. Newspaper cuttings were pinned up along the wall with headlines changing from warnings to searches, then articles that seemed to make fun of Wilfred for claiming the brothers had been attacked by monsters.

Billy's eyes were drawn to a particularly horrible newspaper article with the headline: IS THE KID A LIAR? WAS IT ALL A HOAX? A picture of Wilfred was in that cutting, too.

No wonder Mr Revel is so sad and keeps to himself, Billy thought. *No one believed his story, and some people even* blamed *him for the fact that his brother went missing! But I know he's telling the truth.*

The sound of the back door slamming made them all jump.

Before they knew it, Mr Revel was stumbling towards them, arms raised and a rolling pin clutched in one hand.

'You dirty little scoundrels!' he shouted. 'Can I not even take my bins out without you lot trying to break in? The youth of today! I know who your parents are! Don't think you can get away with robbing this old man without any consequences.' He grabbed Jimmy's arm. 'Come here, you horrible lot. Let's see what the police have to say about this, shall we?'

Quickly, Billy spoke up. 'Mr Revel, please wait – we can explain!'

'Explain away why you're here, trespassing on my property? *Pah!*' Mr Revel said.

'Hang on, Mr Revel! We're here to talk to you about *Bilfred*!' cried Billy, trembling, but determined to deliver the most important news of his life.

Mr Revel stopped in his tracks – he turned to Billy with a face like absolute thunder.

'How dare you come here and mention my brother's name!'

'But we're here to tell you something important,

Mr Revel,' said Anna, jumping in to help Billy.

'W-we've found Bilfred,' stammered Billy.

'How could you taunt me like this? This is my life, not some fantasy story.'

'But he's alive, Mr Revel! He's been a prisoner in the woods all this time. We *found* him!'

Wilfred looked angry and shocked; all the colour drained from his face. 'What are you talking about? The woods were searched and searched after that day. And I trod every inch of it for years looking for my brother. But even I had to accept the truth: he's not there any more.' Wilfred swallowed a sob. 'Those beasts got him. And that awful woman too, who stole my eye! It's my fault we were there, and it's my fault he didn't escape because I ran and ran and left him. But I was so frightened!'

Billy walked slowly over to the old man and put his arm round him.

'It wasn't your fault, Mr Revel – your brother's alive. Let us prove it to you. Bilfred told us something only he would know.'

'Look up the chimney,' said Andy. 'There's a place

where he hid an old biscuit tin.'

'Unless you've found it already?' added Jimmy. 'Otherwise it should still be there. And inside it is something from Bilfred for you.'

Wilfred looked at the children in disbelief.

'Mr Revel, when you were just a kid, grown-ups didn't believe you when you told them about the creatures in the woods and what really happened to your brother,' Billy said, thinking about the newspaper articles on the wall. 'You know that the woods have got secrets – that's why you've always told us to stay away. So now you have to trust us. We're telling you the truth. Look up the chimney, and you'll know we're not liars.'

A glimmer of hope flashed across Wilfred's eye. He dropped the rolling pin and went over to the fireplace. Billy and the others were silent in anticipation.

Wilfred poked his arm up the chimney and rooted around. 'I can't feel anything,' he muttered.

Billy's heart raced. What if the tin had been moved? Fifty years was a long time . . . How would they get Mr Revel to believe them without this proof?

Then, all of a sudden, the old man's eye widened, and he let out a gasp. He wriggled his arm and tugged down hard on something. With a flurry of soot, he pulled a very grubby-looking, blackened tin out from the chimney. He stared at it in shock.

'It can't be . . . it can't be,' he whispered, wiping the top of the tin with his sleeve.

'Bilfred said he was saving it for your tenth birthday,' said Anna.

Gently, Wilfred lifted the lid and peered inside. His whole face lit up and tears welled in his eye as he pulled out a small metal train. He placed it on the table and reached back into the tin, this time removing a handmade card, faded but still clear enough to see the words *To the best big brother in the world* on the front with a drawing of two boys holding hands.

Wilfred passed it to Anna, unable to read it out himself.

'*Wilf! Happy Birthday! I love you more than Eccles cake, love Bilfred*,' she said.

Billy stepped forward. 'See, we're not lying, Mr Revel. We really have found Bilfred. But he can't come to you, so we need to take you to him. He's . . . grown a fair bit since you last saw him.'

Wilfred looked confused. 'I just can't believe all this.'

'Trust us,' said Andy. 'Now, Mr Revel, it smells like your pie might be ready. Do you want to eat?'

Wilfred shook his head in confusion.

'Well, do you mind if I do?' Andy asked. Wilfred nodded, still lost for words, while Andy headed into the kitchen.

'Andy! Now is not the time to eat!' Anna exclaimed.

'Waste not, want not – there's never *not* a good time to eat,' Andy replied, and before anyone could say anything else, he had the pie in hand and was already tucking in. The filling had to be as hot as the centre of the earth, but he had devised a clever way of breathing, chatting and eating that cooled food down super quickly.

Nodding to one of the headlines on the wall, Andy said, 'No offence, Mr Revel, but I never saw you as a singer . . .'

Wilfred looked down and said, 'I haven't sung since the day I lost my brother.' There was silence as no one knew what to say.

Then Andy piped up again, with steam coming out of his nose: 'In life, Mr Revel, some people are faced with terrible things. You and your brother have both suffered greatly since you lost each other, but that brotherly love has never faded. The way I look at it, you've got nothing to lose, so grab your things and come with us.'

Billy, Anna and Jimmy looked at each other in surprise. Yet again, Andy had come out with something completely unexpected and completely brilliant – all while talking with his mouth full.

Billy jumped in, trying to explain further. 'The woods that you've been searching are not the same woods that we know. We've found a window to another world, another woods. The same but very different. I know how weird this sounds, but you said yourself you've been searching these woods for years and never found any trace of Bilfred. We can take you to him.'

Wilfred, lost in thought, simply stated quietly, 'Take me to my brother.'

The four friends followed him through the old iron gate at the end of his property, straight into the woods. As they walked towards the old oak tree to reunite Wilfred with Bilfred, his long-lost brother, after fifty years, they thought, *What could possibly go wrong?*

Chapter 12

Together Again!

Back at the oak tree, Wilfred started to shake.

'This is where I lost him, all those years ago,' he muttered, looking around sadly. 'It all happened so fast. I climbed up this big tree, trying to escape from the beasts and that lady who stole my eye. Waiting for my chance to rescue Bilfred. But a moment later he just vanished into the darkness, and all the howling stopped in an instant.'

'Mr Revel, this tree is the window into the other world we were telling you about,' explained Billy. 'We found our way in by accident when we hugged the tree, and you must have closed it without realizing when you were hiding high up in the branches and holding on to the tree. That's why Bilfred disappeared, and no one could find him.'

'But now we know how to open and close the window,' said Jimmy.

'Are you ready, Mr Revel?' asked Anna gently. Wilfred nodded, so Anna took him by the hand and walked him right up to the tree. 'You need to reach up and give it a hug,' she told him.

Wilfred took a deep breath, shaking his head in disbelief. 'This feels ridiculous.'

'Trust us, Mr Revel. Give it a proper hug,' Billy chipped in. 'You should feel a little tingle. Go on – you need to do it to find your brother.'

Wilfred had come this far, so he shrugged and did exactly what the kids had said. As the tingle went through his body, the old man watched in wonder as everything shifted, and a new world of the woods appeared before him. Just beyond the tree a fire was glowing, a lone silhouette warming its hands by the flames.

Wilfred ran and stumbled towards the glow.

'Bilfred?' he said. 'Bilfred, is it really you?'

Bilfred turned and leapt to his feet, towering over his brother. Their recognition was instant. He reached out and scooped Wilfred up in his arms in the biggest bear hug ever. It was a sight to behold. The two brothers were crying, laughing and pinching each other over and over to check if the other was real. It was a good ten minutes before either of them could string a sentence together, other than Wilfred constantly exclaiming, 'You're so big!'

'I can't believe it's really you,' said Wilfred, staring up at his little brother.

'And me, you,' Bilfred replied. 'Now, I do have a few friends to introduce you to, my bestest big brother. Go on, my little pals. Do that special thing you do when you're happy.'

And, with that, the air around them filled with thousands of glowing Sprites, like twinkling stars dancing in the moonlight.

Wilfred looked on in wonder. 'First you're so big,

and now they're so small,' he squealed in amazement.
'This is all just a dream.'

'Allow me to introduce myself, Wilfred,' said Chief
Mirren, floating to his side. 'I'm Chief Mirren, and this
is our community of Sprites. We would be honoured to
escort you back to our home, Balthazar, to celebrate
this happy and long overdue reunion.'

No one needed to be told twice, and the whole gang
trekked together through the woods, the kids carrying
their flying buzzpacks, guided by the moonlight and the
twinkling glow of the Sprites. Wilfred, Bilfred and the
four friends laughed and chatted the whole way back
to Balthazar. The brothers were so overjoyed to be
together that what was actually a long journey felt like
no time at all.

Hungry and happy, everyone tucked into another
Sprite feast, talking, eating and dancing together.
Afterwards, Billy, Anna, Jimmy and Andy collapsed in
a happy pile and slowly fell asleep to the beautiful
singing of the brothers, duetting together for the first
time since that dark day.

What we've got, we've got each other!
Before this day I'd lost my brother,
But we've found each other now.
I'm just not quite sure how

We'll grow, grow, grow together.
GROW, GROW, GROW!

The next morning, it was time to say goodbye. Operation Overnight might have given the kids a free pass to stay in the woods, but now their families would be expecting them home soon.

'Mr Revel, would you like to come back with us?' Billy asked. 'We can hold you between us as we fly?'

'Actually, I think I might stay for a while,' said Wilfred, who hadn't left Bilfred's side the entire time. 'Now that I've found my brother, I'm not ready to leave him again just yet.'

'You're both welcome to stay with us for as long as you like – this is your home too, after all, Bilfred,' said Chief Mirren.

'We alls will have lots of fun!' said Basil with a huge grin.

'Before you go, human friends, I want to show you something we've found here at Balthazar,' said Chief Mirren.

She led them to a small room with a large round

table filling much of the space. On top of it were the fragments of a cloth map.

'This appears to show our woods, but it seems to extend further than we've ever ventured. As you can see, many pieces are missing.' She pointed to the gaps in the cloth. 'I have completed a few sections by adding fragments of the maps that have been passed down through Sprite generations, but there are many more to find.'

Bilfred poked his head into the room. 'I couldn't help but overhear,' he said, 'and I think I can help you.' He reached into his back pocket and pulled out an old clothbound book. 'This is my gardening bible, and I've always wondered about this . . .'

He pulled off the cover, and the underside of the cloth was a piece of map, matching exactly the style of the one on the table. He unpicked the stitching and handed it to Billy, who moved it round the table until he was able to slot it neatly into a large gap, like a jigsaw puzzle.

'What does this mean?' asked Anna, looking at the chief.

'I'm not sure yet,' Chief Mirren replied. 'Balthazar
proves that there was definitely a time when Sprites
and Giants worked together in harmony, but Bilfred
here is the first Giant we've ever seen.'

'I'm not a Giant!' Bilfred said. 'I just grew big!'

'Well, nevertheless,' continued Chief Mirren, 'the
skeletons you found when you discovered Balthazar
make me feel that something terrible must have
happened here to destroy that peace and wipe out the
Giants. This map may have been destroyed at the
same time. My hope is that we can continue to piece

it back together to help us understand what tore us Sprites and Giants apart, and to uncover the true extent of Waterfall Woods.'

'Look!' interrupted Jimmy, pointing to the newly joined piece of the map. 'That looks like the edge of another walled garden!'

'Does that mean that Bilfred isn't the only person to be trapped?' asked Billy.

'Perhaps it does, Billy,' said the chief. 'But, that may be a mystery for another day. Now, I think you should return home before you are missed. Please do not share your adventures with anyone else and risk the Rhythm being driven offbeat again.'

'We promise,' they all said in unison.

There was lots of hugging and goodbyes, then Billy and the others put on their flying buzzpacks once again and took to the sky.

Back at the pub, there was still excitement in the air from all the recent press and TV activity in the village. Billy found his mum cutting out newspaper clippings

to put up on the wall, nattering away to Jerry Draper the reporter, who seemed to have an extra air of confidence about him now.

'Oh, you're back, love,' Mum said. 'Perfect timing – we've just put all the specials on. Why don't you pick something for your lunch?'

'OK, Mum,' Billy said, climbing up on a comfy bar stool.

'So what'll it be? Fish and chips? Steak and kidney pie? Or a good old-fashioned ploughman's – honey-roast ham, Grandad's pickles and some lovely fresh bread?'

'I think I'll go for a ploughman's, please.' Billy did love a pickle.

'Good choice – just give me a minute.'

Billy slumped on to the bar, suddenly feeling exhausted after the adventure the night before and all the things he, Anna, Jimmy and Andy had been through over the last few weeks. He would never have believed that he, Billy, the boy who was useless at school and always getting things wrong, could have achieved so much. Thank goodness for his friends, old and new – together they'd been able to help reset the Rhythm and reunite Wilfred and Bilfred.

He smiled as his mum placed a big plate of delicious food in front of him, with a few cheeky chips on the side. Billy spent a moment piling ham, pickled onions, crisp lettuce and a few hot chips on to a wedge of spongy granary bread spread with butter. He raised it to his mouth and took a hugely satisfying bite. Delicious!

Munching happily, Billy's mind whirred with everything that had happened and all the secrets that Waterfall Woods still held.

Life in his small, quiet village suddenly seemed much more exciting.

Epilogue

'That can't be the end?' Autumn said, staring at me. 'What happened next? What's going on with the walled gardens? *Are* there more Giants? And what about the two-headed beasts?'

'And who made those flying buzzpacks?' Jesse chipped in.

'That's the end of our adventure for now,' I said. 'All I will say is that sometimes things have to get worse before they get better.'

The twins groaned in frustration.

'And remember: you must never tell anyone about what happened to us in the woods.'

'*Us?*' Autumn said, her mouth wide open. 'Wait, Dad . . . that boy Billy is you? This is about *you*!

So that means your best friend Anna in the story
is Mum!'

'No way! Wow, Dad! And is that how you got
your scars? From the flint necklace?' Jesse asked,
pointing at my chest.

I nodded. 'But that's a story for another day.'

'I wish I could be as brave and smart as you
were,' said Autumn with a sigh.

'But, Autumn,' I said, 'I didn't think I was brave
or smart, but then I found my own way to get things
done – the Billy-Boy Way. You have to stop
worrying and just be yourself. You'll find your own
way, too. But remember: this is all our secret, right?'

I held my little finger out to the twins for a
twinky promise.

'So you'll tell us the rest of the story soon?'
Autumn asked.

'Promise,' I said. 'And I always keep my
promises.'

If they thought that was an adventure, they were
going to love what the Rhythm threw at us next . . .

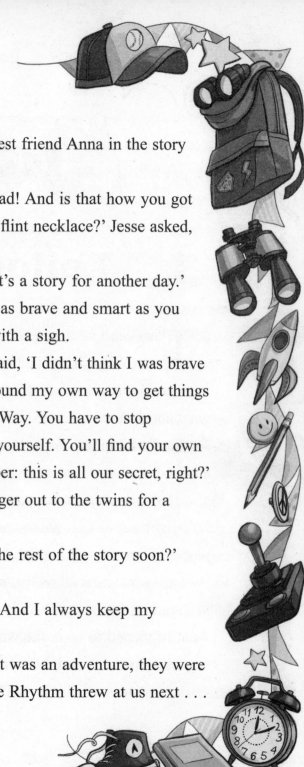

Thank You!

Writing this book has been my passion project and a labour of love. It's taken me four years, but what a journey it's been. I may have written twenty-six cookbooks, but this was an amazing step into the unknown, so I'm forever grateful to everyone who has helped me bring it to life, and I'm so proud of what we've achieved.

First of all, I need to thank Petal, Buddy and River – if you hadn't demanded I make up a bedtime story for you, this would never have happened. And not forgetting Poppy, Daisy and Jools – thank you for your patience!

I also want to thank my JO HQ team. My wonderful, patient editors Rebecca Verity and Rebecca Morten – ladies, it's been a pleasure to work with you. And to my hugely talented creative team James Verity and Barnaby Purdy. Shout-outs to my marketing and PR teams: Tamsyn Zietsman, Rosalind Godber and Michelle Dam. To Sean Moxhay for organizing everyone and keeping us on the straight and narrow. Not to mention Louise Holland, Zoe Collins and Ali Solway. Thank you. It's been a team effort, but it's been worth it!

To the Puffin dream team – you have been so supportive, guiding me all the way. Jane Griffiths, my brilliant editor, you've been amazing (even if you did make me take out a lot of farts!).

And thanks to the brilliant Wendy Shakespeare for her editorial skills too. Ben Hughes is the man with a vision, ably assisted by Janene Spencer. Then to the wider team: Tania Vian-Smith, Phoebe Williams, Roz Hutchinson, Clare Blanchfield, Hannah Sidorjak, Kat Baker, Amy Wilkerson, Alice Grigg, Ruth Knowles and Amanda Punter. Last, but not least, thank you, Francesca Dow, who I felt really understood the heart and soul of this story right from the very beginning.

To the genius illustrator Mónica Armiño – what can I say? Your beautiful drawings have brought the characters and Waterfall Woods to life in the most dynamic way.

When it came to making the audiobook, I've had the pleasure of working with some of the best in the biz. James Keyte, Chris Thompson and Roy McMillan at Penguin Audio, then the dream team at Vaudeville Sound: Dan Jones, Kate 'Bronzie' Bronze, Luke Hatfield, Enzo Cannatella, Lois Green and Zack Marshall. And special shout-outs to the people who brought it all to life: Dexter Fletcher, Jason Flemyng, Amy Wren, Kadeem Ramsay, Benny Mails and Tamzene Allison-Power. Not forgetting star turns from Jools, Buddy and River. Last but not least, a huge thanks to Tobie Tripp and Eleanor Wilson for bringing the music.

BIG LOVE!

Read on for some AMAZING recipes from Jamie Oliver, inspired by Billy's adventure!

These recipes are designed to be made together, so while we hope you have fun cooking up a storm, always make sure you have a grown-up to help you in the kitchen and be very careful around knives and hot ovens.

For nutrition advice and lots more, visit jamieoliver.com/billy.

Pasta and meatballs

with grated courgette, mushroom, onion and garlic

Serves 6

Total time: 1 hour 15 minutes, plus cooling and chilling

1 onion

4 cloves of garlic

1 courgette

6 chestnut mushrooms

olive oil

400g lean minced meat – try beef, pork or a mixture

50g wholemeal breadcrumbs

20g Parmesan cheese

1 large egg

1 x 600g jar of passata

450g dried spaghetti

a handful of fresh basil leaves

1. Peel the onion and 2 cloves of garlic. Coarsely grate them on a box grater with the courgette and mushrooms, then tip it all into a large non-stick frying pan on a medium heat with 1 tablespoon of oil. Cook for 10 minutes, or until softened, stirring occasionally. Tip into a bowl and leave to cool.
2. Add the minced beef, pork and breadcrumbs to the bowl of cooled veg. Finely grate in most of the

Parmesan cheese and crack in the egg, then season with a little black pepper. With clean hands, squish and squash the mixture together until it's all nicely combined. Now wash your hands!

3. With wet hands, take tablespoons of the mixture and shape into 24 even-sized balls. Place them on a tray, cover and pop in the fridge to firm up for 10 minutes or so. Wash your hands again.

4. Place a large non-stick frying pan on a medium heat with 1 teaspoon of oil. Add the meatballs to the pan and cook for 8 to 10 minutes, or until golden and gnarly, turning regularly.

5. While the meatballs are cooking, peel and finely chop the remaining 2 garlic cloves. Create a little space in the pan between the meatballs, add the garlic for 2 minutes, then pour in the passata.

6. Give the pan a gentle shake so the balls are evenly coated in the sauce. Simmer for 30 minutes, or until the meatballs are cooked through and the sauce is thick and delicious, stirring occasionally.

7. About 15 minutes before you're ready to serve, cook the pasta in a large pan of boiling salted water according to the packet instructions, then drain and divide between your plates. Spoon over the meatballs and sauce, and top with a few pretty basil leaves.

Hot chocolate

spiked with cinnamon

Serves 8

Total time: 10 minutes

2 pints of semi-skimmed milk

HOT CHOCOLATE MIX

2 tablespoons Horlicks

2 tablespoons cornflour

3 tablespoons icing sugar

4 tablespoons quality cocoa powder

1 pinch of ground cinnamon

100g quality dark chocolate (70%)

1. Pour the milk into a large pan, and bring almost to the boil over a medium heat.
2. Meanwhile, add all the chocolate mix ingredients to a large jar, finely grating in the chocolate, then give it a good shake to combine.
3. You need around 10 heaped tablespoons of the chocolate mix for this amount of milk. Simply spoon

the chocolate mix into the hot milk, give it a good whisk and leave to bubble away in the pan for a few minutes before serving – you're looking for that gorgeous, thick (almost claggy), knockout texture.

Perfect porridge

with a caramelly glaze

Serves 4

Total time: 20 minutes

1 big builder's mug of coarse rolled large porridge
oats (50g/person)
1 good splash of cold whole milk or cream, plus more
for serving
4 teaspoons granulated brown sugar

1. Place the rolled oats into a high-sided pan with
    3 cups of boiling water and a pinch of salt.
2. Place the pan on a medium heat until it starts to
    boil, then reduce to a simmer for 15 minutes, or
    until thick and creamy, stirring regularly.
3. Add a good splash of whole milk or cream towards
    the end to enrich the porridge and make
    it super-luxurious.
4. Ladle the porridge into wide bowls and leave for
    3 minutes for the residual chill of the
    bowl to slightly cool down the

porridge from the outside in, so it remains soft, silky and oozy in the middle but goes almost firm and jellified around the edges.

5. Sprinkle 1 teaspoon of granulated brown sugar (or to taste) over each bowl and wait 1½ minutes for it to pull out the moisture from the porridge and turn it into a caramelly glaze.

6. Using a butter knife, cut the porridge into a chequerboard pattern. Take your cold whole milk, rest the bottle on the edge of the bowl and gently pour it in, so it fills every crack of the pattern. Then dive straight in.

Jazz it up

- Lightly toast some sunflower, sesame and poppy seeds, crush them in a pestle and mortar with a pinch of ground cinnamon, mix them with some chopped dried fruit, then fold through.

- Or sprinkle seasonal berries with a pinch of sugar and a little lemon juice and stir them through the porridge.

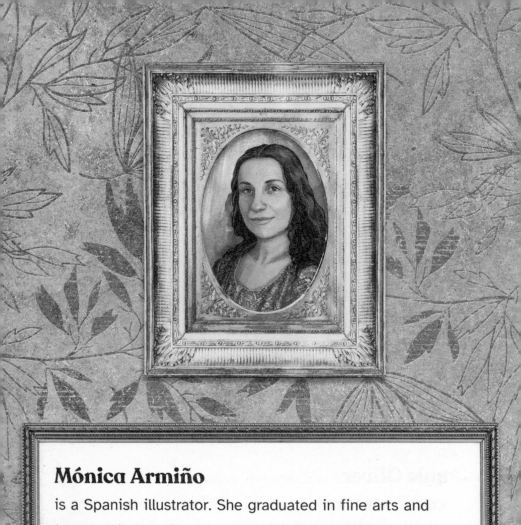

Mónica Armiño

is a Spanish illustrator. She graduated in fine arts and is based in Madrid. She has published several books with various publishers and agencies in Europe and the USA. Mónica also works in the animation industry as a character designer, background artist and colour and texture artist for feature films and pre-school TV series such as the award-winning *Puffin Rock*.

Jamie Oliver

is a global phenomenon in food and campaigning, selling over 48 million books worldwide. He started cooking at his parents' pub (the inspiration for the Green Giant in this book!) at the age of eight. When he left school, Jamie began a career as a chef that led him to the River Café, where he was spotted by a TV producer. Jamie now lives in Essex with his wife Jools and their five children.

Are you ready to step into the world of Waterfall Woods?

Listen to *Billy and the Giant Adventure*,

narrated by Jamie Oliver

alongside a cast of brilliant voices,

with immersive music and sound effects!

Jamie Oliver

Billy
and the
GIANT
Adventure

Where will the fragments
of the map lead?

Who is the mysterious
woman who kidnapped
Bilfred?

What *other* secrets are
waiting to be discovered
in Waterfall Woods?

Don't miss Billy's next adventure! Coming 2024...

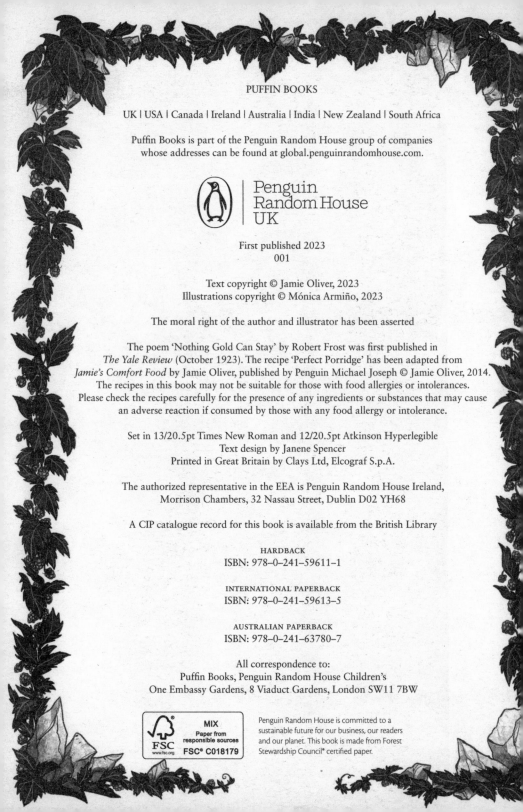

PUFFIN BOOKS

UK | USA | Canada | Ireland | Australia | India | New Zealand | South Africa

Puffin Books is part of the Penguin Random House group of companies
whose addresses can be found at global.penguinrandomhouse.com.

Penguin
Random House
UK

First published 2023
001

Text copyright © Jamie Oliver, 2023
Illustrations copyright © Mónica Armiño, 2023

The moral right of the author and illustrator has been asserted

The poem 'Nothing Gold Can Stay' by Robert Frost was first published in
The Yale Review (October 1923). The recipe 'Perfect Porridge' has been adapted from
Jamie's Comfort Food by Jamie Oliver, published by Penguin Michael Joseph © Jamie Oliver, 2014.
The recipes in this book may not be suitable for those with food allergies or intolerances.
Please check the recipes carefully for the presence of any ingredients or substances that may cause
an adverse reaction if consumed by those with any food allergy or intolerance.

Set in 13/20.5pt Times New Roman and 12/20.5pt Atkinson Hyperlegible
Text design by Janene Spencer
Printed in Great Britain by Clays Ltd, Elcograf S.p.A.

The authorized representative in the EEA is Penguin Random House Ireland,
Morrison Chambers, 32 Nassau Street, Dublin D02 YH68

A CIP catalogue record for this book is available from the British Library

HARDBACK
ISBN: 978–0–241–59611–1

INTERNATIONAL PAPERBACK
ISBN: 978–0–241–59613–5

AUSTRALIAN PAPERBACK
ISBN: 978–0–241–63780–7

All correspondence to:
Puffin Books, Penguin Random House Children's
One Embassy Gardens, 8 Viaduct Gardens, London SW11 7BW